HAS LISA BITTEN OFF
MORE THAN SHE CAN CHEW?

Lisa pulled up beside the barn doors and jumped off. She buried her face in Prancer's neck, sobbing. Seeing her standing there, Red O'Malley put down the bale of hay he was carrying and went to find out what was wrong.

"I'll put Prancer away for you. You just try to calm yourself," he told Lisa, taking the mare's reins.

Lisa was too upset to protest. All day—all week—she had been on the brink of bursting into tears. Veronica's comment had been the last straw. She had been trying her hardest to please everyone, and instead it seemed as if all she got was criticism from every side.

What could she do now? She was so confused, she couldn't think straight anymore. She had to get away—from Pine Hollow, Willow Creek Community Theater, everything. Choking back tears, Lisa ran blindly toward the woods behind the barn as fast as she could. . . .

THE SADDLE CLUB

STAGE
COACH

BONNIE BRYANT

A SKYLARK BOOK®

NEW YORK • TORONTO • LONDON • SYDNEY • AUCKLAND

RL 5, 009–012

STAGE COACH

A Skylark Book / October 1994

Skylark Books is a registered trademark of Bantam Books,
a division of Bantam Doubleday Dell Publishing Group, Inc.
Registered in U.S. Patent and Trademark Office and elsewhere.

"The Saddle Club" is a trademark of Bonnie Bryant Hiller.
The Saddle Club design / logo, which consists of an inverted
U-shaped design, a riding crop, and a riding hat is a
trademark of Bantam Books.

ISBN 0-553-48153-3

Published simultaneously in the United States and Canada

Bantam Books are published by Bantam Books, a division of Bantam Doubleday Dell Publishing Group, Inc. Its trademark, consisting of the words
"Bantam Books" and the portrayal of a rooster, is Registered in U.S. Patent
and Trademark Office and in other countries. Marca Registrada. Bantam
Books, 1540 Broadway, New York, New York 10036.

PRINTED IN THE UNITED STATES OF AMERICA

CWO   0 9 8 7 6 5 4 3 2 1

I would like to express my special thanks to Caitlin C. Macy for her help in the writing of this book.

LISA ATWOOD SWUNG open the doors to Pine Hollow with a flourish. She was always eager to get to the stable where she and her two best friends, Carole Hanson and Stevie Lake, rode, helped out, and generally hung around having fun, but today she was practically bursting with news to share.

Whenever any member of The Saddle Club had something exciting happen to her—whether good or bad —her first instinct was to tell the others. Stevie, Carole, and Lisa had started The Saddle Club as a group for horse-crazy people like themselves, but that wasn't the only requirement for joining. They also had to stick together through thick and thin by being willing to help each other out in all kinds of situations.

Lisa found Carole and Stevie right away. They were removing their tack from the tack room to get ready for the Horse Wise mounted meeting that would begin soon. Horse Wise was the name of the local Pony Club. Luckily for the girls, its home base was Pine Hollow, and so meetings were almost always held there.

"You're never going to believe what just happened to me!" Lisa cried.

Stevie and Carole paused with their bridles and saddles in hand. "You ran into Skye Ransom at the mall and invited him over to Pony Club," Stevie suggested, grinning.

"I only wish," Lisa replied, sighing at the young movie star's name. Actually, Stevie's guess wasn't as far-fetched as it sounded. Once The Saddle Club *had* run into Skye Ransom, on a trip they took to New York. They had helped him out with his riding for a movie, and he had rewarded them by inviting them to appear in bit parts in the film. "But, no," Lisa continued, "he wasn't hanging out at the Willow Creek Mall. Guess again."

"You got a call from the United States Equestrian Team headquarters, and they've picked you for the Olympic team," Carole ventured.

"Yeah, in my dreams, maybe." Lisa laughed.

"All right, we give up. So what happened?" Stevie asked.

Lisa smiled. "Thought you'd never ask. Actually, it has nothing to do with horses at all."

Carole and Stevie exchanged glances. What on earth could have excited Lisa so much if horses weren't involved? Unless maybe a boy—

"*Or* boys," Lisa said, reading her friends' minds. "Although I do think that Skye Ransom would probably be pleased to hear that I'm going to be performing once again." She paused to heighten the suspense. Then she blurted out all at once, "I got cast in the lead role in *Annie* at the Willow Creek Community Theater!"

Stevie and Carole stared at her. "You mean *you're* Annie?" Carole asked incredulously.

"That's right," Lisa said. "I thought I was only going to get a chorus part—or maybe one of the orphans—but I kept getting called back for more auditions. Finally it came down to me and one other girl. I was so nervous, I was shaking! I had to sing and dance and read lines with Mr. Ryan—he's that old guy who's in all the musicals, and he's playing Daddy Warbucks—and I messed up twice! It was so embarrassing. I forgot the words to our duet, and he had to mouth them to me, but I kept remembering what my mother told me, keep smiling, no matter what—and after a while they told the other girl to go, and they told me I got the part! *The* part!" Lisa paused to catch her breath.

"That's great, Lisa. Congratulations," Carole said.

3

Stevie stared into space reflectively. "I can see your name up in lights: 'Lisa Atwood, star of stage and screen —and stable'!" she joked.

"So when do rehearsals start?" Carole asked.

Lisa grinned. "This afternoon—I can hardly wait," she replied, giving herself an excited hug.

Carole looked slightly taken aback. "Wow, today, huh?" she repeated.

"I guess the show must go on, right, Lisa?" Stevie asked, trying to sound supportive.

Lisa looked from one to the other. "You guys don't sound all that thrilled," she commented.

Carole was the first to reply. "It's not that we're not excited for you, it's just that—well, I, for one, had no idea you were even auditioning. I guess I didn't even know you were really interested in acting. I'm just a little surprised that it's all happening so fast."

Lisa nodded. Part of what Carole said was true. She had been secretive about the auditions—not because she hadn't wanted to tell Carole and Stevie, but because she felt shy about wanting to be in the play at all. "I know I didn't tell you," she said. "I didn't want to make a big deal of it unless I got in. I figured I'd surprise you with the news."

Before she could say anything further, Max Regnery's voice boomed over the stable intercom. "Horse Wise will meet in the indoor ring in ten minutes. Please be

4

ready to present your mount for a routine tack-and-turn-out check. Nothing fancy, I just want to make sure you've been keeping up with your grooming and tack cleaning."

The Saddle Club immediately split up and headed for their horses' stalls. When the owner of Pine Hollow and the head instructor of Horse Wise said "routine," everyone knew he meant "extremely picky."

As Lisa went about grooming and tacking up, she couldn't help humming some warm-up scales and a few bars of "Tomorrow." She could hardly believe she was going to be up onstage, singing solo in front of hundreds of people. The thought of singing made her want to burst out in song. She was bubbling over with excitement. Besides, Ellen Spitz, the musical director, had told her to practice as much as she could to improve her breathing.

"Mi-mi-mi-mi-mi-mi-mi-mi-mi," she sang softly as she placed the saddle on the horse's back. "Do-re-mi-fa-so-la-ti-do!" On the last note she let herself sing out a bit. Guiltily, she glanced down the row of stalls. She knew horses hated loud noises. Sure enough, the ears on every head had gone back. Maybe she didn't have to practice *all* the time.

Stevie and Carole stopped to collect Lisa for the meeting. The three of them liked to meet before Horse Wise, even for a couple of minutes, to try to predict faults Max would find with their turnout—shavings in a tail, a crooked saddle pad, dirty boots. Today Lisa's oversight was a little easier to spot. Carole and Stevie lost no time in pointing it out.

"Uh, Lisa, were you planning to ride Prancer today?" Stevie asked, giggling.

Lisa spun around. In her excitement she had tacked up the Thoroughbred mare instead of Barq, her usual Pony Club mount. She laughed out loud at her empty-headedness. "I guess this *Annie* thing is getting to me," she admitted. "On second thought, though, I am just as happy to ride Prancer." Lisa had been on the ex-racehorse many times before and had even schooled her for a horse show. Lately she had stuck with the more reliable Barq for Pony Club—which usually included jumping—and had ridden Prancer only on the flat. The mare could be a handful around other horses and over fences. Today Lisa felt up to a challenge, though.

Stevie echoed her thoughts. "Max will be glad you're challenging yourself, and anyway, I heard him say we're not going to jump this afternoon."

"Boy, I don't know what's going on at all," Lisa said. "I wonder why we're not jumping. I've been so caught up in the play. . . ." She let her voice trail off, thinking about the frenzied past week of auditions and callbacks.

"Lisa, you look so worried, you *could* be an orphan in

6

an orphanage," Stevie kidded, breaking through her thoughts.

Lisa smiled. The nerve-racking, nail-biting week was over. She had gotten the lead role, and she was here at Pine Hollow with her two best friends about to ride one of her favorite horses. "I was just thinking about how worried I've been about tryouts and everything," she admitted.

"Hey, you're serious about acting, aren't you?" Carole asked with admiration.

"Look," Lisa said, seizing the chance to explain, "I'm not saying I want to run away to Broadway, but I'm flattered I got the part, and I'm going to give it a shot. And I forgot to tell you, there are still a few chorus roles left—why don't you guys join the troupe? It would be so much fun if we were all in it."

Carole and Stevie burst out laughing at the thought of themselves in a play.

"Yeah, right," Stevie said. "Imagine me trying to sing! My brothers yell at me when I hum in the shower!"

"I know. And think of me trying to get up in front of an audience. I'd forget my lines so fast, they'd think I had laryngitis," Carole said.

When Lisa started to think about it, she had to laugh, too. Stevie wasn't exactly known for her sweet soprano, and Carole could be totally disorganized and shy when it came to anything but horses. Lisa had seen her walking around school with an overstuffed notebook, bumping into people and leaving a trail of paper behind her.

"Even though we couldn't be in the play to save our lives, we'll definitely come watch," Carole assured her.

"Absolutely—front-row seats," Stevie said.

"Oh, don't worry, I already bought tickets for you guys," Lisa said.

"When is the performance, anyway? Do you have months and months of rehearsals?" Stevie asked.

"I'm not sure," Lisa said. "But I do know that Mrs. Spitz's philosophy is to rehearse very intensely so that the cast really gets to know one another. I'll probably have to spend a lot of time there."

"So this might be your last Horse Wise meeting for a while?" Carole asked.

"Last Horse Wise!" Lisa looked at her with surprise. "Are you kidding? There's no way I would ever give up riding for the play."

"But how are you going to do both?" Carole asked.

"*And* keep up your grades?" Stevie added. They all knew that keeping up her straight-A average was important to Lisa.

Lisa relaxed. She had been anticipating both questions and had answers ready. In the car on the way over, she had mapped out a daily schedule of school, homework, chores, riding, and rehearsing. She eagerly produced the piece of paper from her pocket. "Look, you guys, it's perfect," she said.

Stevie and Carole looked. It was perfect—in a Lisa Atwood kind of way. It was a typical Lisa masterpiece. She had fine-tuned her day down to the minute.

"Eight minutes for dinner, huh?" Stevie commented.

Lisa nodded brightly. "Exactly eight minutes. That ought to be perfect. And then I can help Mom with the dishes for two minutes, see—right there." Lisa pointed to the tiny boxed-in square between "Dinner" and "Math Homework." "And notice that I'll be here for every Horse Wise Saturday meeting and our riding lesson every Tuesday."

Stevie and Carole pored over the schedule, ignoring Topside and Starlight, who were moving around restlessly. Both of them had noticed that Lisa hadn't mentioned Saddle Club time, or time for going to TD's, the ice-cream parlor that was their favorite hangout—let alone chore time at Pine Hollow.

By their puzzled expressions Lisa knew what they were thinking. "Look, it's true that I won't have any extra time to spend at Pine Hollow—riding or doing chores—and I'll have to see you on Tuesdays and Saturdays instead of all the time. But this play is really important to me. I have to give up *something*. I had to beg Mrs. Spitz just to skip two Tuesday choreography sessions so that I

9

could be here." Lisa looked at Stevie and Carole to see how they were taking her explanation.

"All right, I guess we'll see you twice a week, then," Stevie said. Her voice sounded glum, though she made an effort to smile.

"What about talking? Can't we even call you?" Carole asked. "It looks like there's an empty block between 'Math' and 'Social Studies Homework.'"

"Right—that's fourteen whole minutes. I put it there specifically so that I could talk to both of you. Isn't that great?"

"Yeah, great," Stevie muttered. "Can I get a copy of the schedule so I can make sure to call exactly at nine-twelve?" she asked sarcastically.

Lisa stared at her blankly. "Sure, Stevie, I'd be happy to give you one," she said.

Once again Max's voice interrupted their conversation. This time, though, it was in person, not over an intercom. He strode down the aisle past the three of them, tapping his crop against his boots. "Horse Wise begins in twenty seconds. Boy, am I glad I'll be on time," he murmured to himself, looking straight ahead.

For the first time the girls could remember, Max's interruption actually came as a relief.

IN A MATTER of minutes the Pony Clubbers had passed inspection more or less successfully and were mounted and walking on a loose rein. Except for the fact that Lisa was riding Prancer, it was the usual group. Veronica was on her Arabian, Garnet; Polly Giacomin was riding her new brown gelding, Romeo; Betsy Cavanaugh sat astride Pine Hollow's Comanche.

Stevie took the opportunity of Max's turned back to catch up to Carole and whisper a question. "Do you think she's serious about this?" she asked as Topside drew along Starlight.

Carole didn't have to ask who "she" or "this" was. At the other end of the ring, Lisa was singing again. This time she had launched into "It's a Hard-Knock Life" and had already repeated the chorus twice. The other students in the class, as well as Max, were starting to give her funny looks.

"Yes, I do think she's serious about it. She's probably trying to practice singing while she warms up to save time," Carole pointed out. "I heard her telling Max about the schedule on the way in. He didn't seem thrilled."

"I just hope she doesn't take things too far," Stevie said.

"I think singing at Pony Club might be a little too far already," Carole said.

Stevie followed Carole's glance to the end of the ring. Max, too, was staring intently at Lisa and didn't looked pleased. He had his arms folded across his chest and was shaking his head. He started to say something and then seemed to think better of it. Instead he burst into song. "Today-ay, today-ay, we're riding today, Lisa Atwood, you're miles away!"

Nobody in the class had ever heard Max sing before. They burst into laughter when they heard him making fun of Lisa in his gravelly baritone.

At the sound of her name Lisa snapped back to reality. She turned toward Max, grinning sheepishly. "Sorry, Max, I guess I was kind of distracted."

Max half smiled. "Just try to forget about 'Tomorrow' while it's today, all right? Class will run a lot more smoothly if we all do one thing at a time," he said. More quietly he added, "Don't make me wish I had taken you off Prancer, Lisa."

Lisa reprimanded herself inwardly. She knew she had been lucky to escape with only a ribbing from Max. Next time tuning out during Pony Club would mean a lecture after class or some harsh, embarrassing words. Max was a stickler for paying full attention. And he was right to warn her about Prancer—the Thoroughbred was no mount for a beginner or for anyone who was going to get distracted. Max had liked the idea of Lisa's being back on Prancer. She didn't want him to regret it. She vowed to work especially hard in the lesson. And she would start by tuning in to the announcement Max had just begun.

". . . so you may think you're in for a relaxing lesson. Well, think again. Just because we're not going to jump today doesn't mean you can take it easy. Get ready for some intense dressage schooling. All right, back out to the rail. Lisa, you lead off. Everyone follow, leaving two horse lengths behind the horse in front of you."

As she took her place at the front of the line, Lisa glanced back quickly at Carole and Stevie. The two of them rolled their eyes. When it came to dressage, Max could be even more demanding than usual. Basically, The Saddle Club knew, dressage meant schooling on the flat and not over fences. But to Max it meant more. Like

13

a good dressage judge, he expected to see horse and rider working together calmly and fluidly, with no sign of struggle.

For the next forty-five minutes he drilled the six riders nonstop. He began by keeping them at a sitting trot for ten minutes, barking out a stream of commands. "Stevie, elbows close to your sides, and stop playing the piano with your hands. Lisa, it's no wonder Prancer just broke into a canter—your inside leg is stiff and it's banging against her. Betsy, shorten up your reins—Comanche's all strung out. Relax your shoulders, Carole, and bring them back. Polly, you're riding too close to Starlight— Romeo looks miserable. If that's a sitting trot, Veronica, I'd like to see what posting looks like. Okay, on the count of three, halt. One, two, three."

Max paused and looked down the line of riders carefully. Every rider sat still and prayed that her horse wouldn't fidget. "That's on the count of *three*, Betsy, not seventeen!" he snapped. "And I only see two people who are square in front—Lisa and Stevie. Everyone else gets about a three for this part of the test."

Except for Lisa and Stevie, who grinned to themselves, the class grimaced as a whole. Max was grading them by the system dressage judges used to evaluate different sections of dressage tests. Every dressage test was divided into sections of different prescribed movements, and these movements were marked on a scale of one to ten. No matter what the level of test, beginner or grand prix, one movement was always the same: The rider was required to halt at the beginning and end of the test to salute the judge. A good halt was very important—it started the ride off on the right foot, and it left a positive, final impression. And one of the most important aspects of a good halt was that the horse's feet be square, or even, at least in front if not all around. Obviously, Max was disappointed to see that only two people had halted correctly.

"Lisa and Stevie," he said, after he had asked everyone to pick up a trot again, "would you mind explaining how you achieved your halting success?"

"I tried to look good and figured Topside would do the rest," Stevie said honestly. Everyone laughed. It was well-known that Topside was one of the most perfectly schooled horses at Pine Hollow. He had been a top-level show horse for years. His owner, championship rider Dorothy DeSoto Hawthorne, had donated him to the farm after a bad fall left her grounded.

Because of his training, riding Topside was a treat. He not only behaved beautifully and had wonderful gaits, he also seemed to understand what Max was saying half the time. Often Stevie would be about to ask him to trot or canter, only to find he'd already picked up the new gait himself, having understood Max's command.

When the laughter had died down, Max asked Lisa to

answer his question. "We all know stopping isn't the first thing they teach at the track," he added, referring to Prancer's previous life as a racehorse.

Lisa thought hard. She wasn't sure what to say, and she could hardly believe Prancer was listening to her so well. "I think I just thought 'Please halt, Prancer,' and then she did," Lisa said. It sounded strange to admit, but she hadn't been conscious of asking the mare to do anything special.

Max nodded approvingly. "Exactly what I was hoping someone would say. A lot of the time we get nervous about halting, and we start fiddling with the reins and leaning way back and doing all kinds of unnecessary things. What we should do is *relax* into a halt—think 'halt,' as Lisa said, and let our bodies do the rest unconsciously."

"But, Max," Stevie joked, "I thought this lesson wasn't supposed to be relaxing."

Max gave her a withering look and continued the lesson.

WHEN THEY DISMOUNTED half an hour later, a buzz went through the group about the day's lesson. The Saddle Club members, for their part, were sure something was up. Max had been so full of instructions for each rider that it was obvious he cared a lot about how well the group was doing. Normally he was fussy, but today he seemed to be testing them to see how fast they could respond to his criticisms.

As they stood rolling up their stirrups and loosening their girths, Max came over and asked Lisa to hold off for a minute. Without a word he took Prancer's reins, lengthened the stirrups to his own level, and sprang up into the saddle. "If you'll all stay at the end of the ring and watch, this will only take a few minutes."

Horse Wise didn't need to be asked twice. They loved watching Max ride but hardly ever got to. He did his own schooling at dawn or earlier and taught the rest of the day.

Max had halted Prancer in the middle of the ring. He removed his hat and crisply saluted an imaginary judge. Horse Wise watched spellbound as horse and rider went through the rest of the dressage test. Max hardly moved as he asked Prancer to lengthen her trot, canter in small circles, and leg-yield down the diagonals. The mare's ears turned forward and back, listening to his imperceptible signals. Finally they turned down the center line a second time. Once again Max halted and saluted. This time Stevie seized the moment. She led Topside away from the group and smartly saluted Max back. The minute Max smiled and relaxed the reins, the whole class burst into applause.

"Lunch on the knoll by the back pasture in twenty minutes," Max said, trying unsuccessfully to cut short

17

the clapping. He dismounted, led Prancer back over to Lisa, and turned over the reins. "You've really got her going nicely, Lisa," he said. Lisa didn't wait for him to leave before high-fiving her friends.

WHEN THE HORSES had been untacked, groomed, watered, and hayed, the riders gathered with their bag lunches on the knoll Max had mentioned. The warm sun shining down only increased their sense of well-being.

"There's nothing better than a good, hard ride and then lunch, is there?" Carole asked.

With their mouths full of sandwiches, Stevie and Lisa could only nod. They found themselves eating faster than usual, partly out of hunger but partly out of excitement about Max's performance and what it meant.

Lisa, meanwhile, was glad to have the excuse of eating so that she didn't have to talk. She couldn't totally join in the excitement, because she had a sinking feeling in the pit of her stomach that whatever Max told them, it would make her perfect schedule a little less perfect.

"I'll bet there's a dressage rider coming to give a clinic," Betsy Cavanaugh guessed.

"I'll bet Veronica's father is buying her an imported German dressage horse," Stevie muttered. To The Saddle Club's delight, Veronica's chauffeur had appeared to whisk her away right after class. The rich, spoiled girl often left Horse Wise right after the riding was over.

"It's better than either of those," Max said. He had come up behind them and was listening to their talk with an amused expression. "At least I think so."

The group fell silent immediately. Making his voice sound casual, Max asked, "Anybody want to go to a rally?"

There was a pause as everyone tried to make sense of Max's question. What was the big news about going to rally? Horse Wise entered a team every year, and, anyway, it didn't come until the summer. "Max, rally's not until next year," Carole pointed out. "And we were already planning on going, weren't we?"

Max smiled. "That's true, Carole—combined training rally isn't until next June. But *dressage* rally is the first Saturday of next month—two weeks away!"

Before Max could fill in any details, everyone began talking at once. Horse Wise had never sent teams to the more specialized Pony Club regional competitions—dressage rally and show-jumping rally—partly because it was simply too hard to find the practice time. Also, a lot of riders, including The Saddle Club, were busy with riding events outside of Pony Club, like horse shows, trail riding, and fox hunting. Finally, and most important, both Max and his mother, Mrs. Reg, who helped run Pine Hollow, felt it was more important for students to ride as much as they could than to compete as much as they could. They thought too much competition made riders lose track of the real purpose of their sport—learning to be good horsemen and horsewomen.

"Yes, it's a change," Max said, his voice rising over the excited chatter. "But I'll tell you why I think it's a good one. First of all, it will be great practice for the dressage part of combined training rally. Second, it will be a new challenge for you. And finally, I know you'll all work like crazy for the next two weeks and prove my hunch that you deserve to go. You've got the potential," Max finished, looking directly at The Saddle Club. "I want to see the results."

After the talk had died down again, Max supplied the rest of the information. Since there were six qualified dressage riders at Horse Wise—Carole, Stevie, Lisa, Polly, Betsy, and Veronica—but only four riders to a team, Horse Wise would have to split up. Four riders would compete as one team, representing Horse Wise alone, while the other two would join two riders from another club.

"For instance," Max went on, "if, say, Cross County Pony Club has a couple of extra riders, we could join with them." Max grinned wickedly at The Saddle Club. Even he knew that Stevie's boyfriend, Phil, was a member of Cross County.

As she listened, Lisa tried to look as happy about the news as everyone else. It was hard not to worry, though. Preparing for the rally meant there would be extra riding practices, as well as meetings to get all the tack, equipment, and clothes ready for inspection. And in the final couple of days, there would be the usual flurry of bathing, mane pulling, and metal polishing. Each rider would also have to memorize the two dressage tests she would ride.

"This afternoon I would like you all to check with Mrs. Reg to see what level test you'll be riding," Max stated. "That depends on your rating. D-threes obviously don't ride the same tests as C-threes. Then go and walk through your tests in the indoor ring—unmounted. It may sound silly, but it'll give you a foundation and get you started thinking about the movements. Check the office before you go—I'm going to post a 'Countdown to Dressage Rally' schedule."

Max folded the list he'd been consulting. "You'll also have to choose a stable manager to oversee the process of getting the equipment ready," he said. "That might be a good job for one of the younger riders. Have fun preparing, girls."

As he turned toward the barn, he took Lisa aside. "Lisa, I'll bet I know why you look worried," he said. "And I agree, it's a difficult choice."

Lisa looked up at him, surprised. She hadn't been prepared for Max to be understanding about her conflict between activities. As far as she knew, he didn't have a great passion for the stage. Maybe he was going to let her

21

miss some lessons or come late some of the time. "I just don't know what to do," Lisa admitted.

"I know," Max said. "So I'm going to tell you what I think: You should ride Prancer at the rally instead of Barq."

"But—" Lisa tried to interrupt.

"You've come a long way with her," Max was saying "and that was clear to me today. In the end she'll be a better dressage horse than Barq. And if you want to start riding her in Pony Club, there's no better time than the present." Max shook his head. "I wouldn't have believed she was the same horse that you took to the show. Besides, I think Betsy would do nicely on Barq. She had a lot of trouble with Comanche today."

Lisa smiled wanly. It should have been music to her ears to hear that, as a direct result of The Saddle Club's working with her, Prancer had changed from the flighty, nervous mare who had once kicked a judge at a local show. Instead Lisa felt a sense of dread. It was confirmed by Max's parting words: "Two weeks of solid practice, and I know you two can really get it together. Just remember, between now and the rally, every minute counts."

"Right," Lisa mumbled. Pensively she crumpled up her lunch bag, watching Max walk away.

"What's up?" Stevie inquired as she and Carole joined Lisa.

"Oh, it's—nothing, really," Lisa answered. She didn't feel like getting into the whole thing just then, especially when Carole and Stevie looked so excited.

"So let's get to it—I want to go talk to Mrs. Reg right away," Carole said.

"Me, too," Stevie agreed. "I can't wait to find out what test I have. How 'bout you, Lisa?"

Lisa looked up, lost in thought. "Me? Well, I—I—" She paused, looking down at her watch. "Oh, my gosh— I have a rehearsal in fourteen minutes! I'll barely make it if I run all the way!" She took off in the direction of the driveway. "I'll call you tonight!"

"At nine-twelve?" Stevie yelled after her.

"Yes! I mean, no! I don't know! I have to rearrange my whole schedule!" Lisa yelled back. As an afterthought she stopped and called, "Hey, if I get out early, I'll come back and practice!"

Watching her run toward the driveway, Stevie and Carole sighed in unison. For some reason they were getting a bad feeling about the play.

EVEN THOUGH SHE ran all the way, practically knocking people over on the sidewalks, and taking a shortcut through the soccer fields, Lisa was nearly ten minutes late to rehearsal. As she ran, she prayed that Mrs. Spitz and the rest of the cast would be singing a big chorus number so that they might not notice her late arrival.

With a final gasp of exhaustion, she banged through the doors of the auditorium at the high school, where the theater staged its productions. Ten heads turned from the stage. Ten pairs of eyes stared at Lisa. Lisa gulped. "I—I—sorry I'm late," she mumbled finally.

To her dismay Lisa noticed that Mrs. Spitz wasn't even seated at the practice piano. So much for a loud song masking her entrance. As quietly as she could, Lisa mounted the stairs to the stage. Mrs. Spitz motioned for her to squeeze her way into the circle of actors. "Hello, Lisa. You're late, as I'm sure you're aware, so I'll fill you in, but please don't make it a habit. The principals are doing a read-through today. I've been reading your part. We're on page seven."

Lisa licked her lips. Her throat felt dry. "The principals? Are doing a read-through?" she repeated timidly.

Mrs. Spitz smiled. "That's right. All the 'principals'—the actors with lead roles—are 'reading through' the script. I forgot that you're new to WCCT. That's what we call Willow Creek Community Theater."

Lisa blushed crimson. Here she was at her first rehearsal—late and making a fool out of herself because she didn't understand the dramatic lingo.

"Yes, with a voice like that, it's easy to forget that you haven't had much experience on the stage, Lisa," someone said. Lisa looked up gratefully. Mr. Ryan, who was playing Daddy Warbucks and had been in umpteen WCCT productions, was smiling encouragingly at her. Lisa tried to smile back. Inwardly she told herself not to feel bad—to cheer up and make the most of the rehearsal. She looked cautiously around the group, pleased to see a bunch of kids her own age.

Before Lisa could relax any more, though, another pang of embarrassment hit her. She had forgotten her script. She could see it in her mind, lying at the bottom of her locker at Pine Hollow where she had left it that morning. She had been planning to grab it on her way out. Max's announcement and having to rush over had completely wiped out any other thought. Against her will hot tears welled up in her eyes. Late, inexperienced, and now this!

Grimly, Lisa gritted her teeth. There was only one way out—she would have to look on with someone. She stole a glance at the girl on her left. To her relief she recognized the girl who had been at the final audition for the role of Annie. She had evidently been cast as an orphan. Telling herself that they at least sort of knew each other, Lisa whispered, "Could I share with you?" The girl shrugged and held her script slightly away from her so that Lisa could see—barely.

Before long Lisa's mood had changed from embarrassment to annoyance. She had to crane her neck so hard it was starting to hurt, and what was more, every few minutes the girl with the script gave a loud "sniff." The rest of the time she held her nose conspicuously away from Lisa. Lisa knew the reason for her rude behavior, and she didn't like it one bit: If there was one thing Lisa and the whole Saddle Club hated, it was people who didn't like horses. True, Lisa hadn't had time to shower and change after Horse Wise—if she had, she would have remembered her script and wouldn't have had to look on, anyway—but it wasn't as if she smelled like a wet dog or skunk or something really disgusting.

The girl also kept staring at Lisa's breeches and boots as if she were wearing a space suit. Lisa decided to stare right back, in between lines. She knew it was rude, but she was so annoyed from running to make it to rehearsal that she was practically past caring.

Orphan, Lisa thought to herself. She's not an orphan for nothing! Her private joke cheered her up a little, but she wished Stevie and Carole were there to share it. They wouldn't have liked the orphan either.

At the ten-minute break, while the other cast members talked to one another and got drinks from the water fountain, Lisa stayed onstage. She lay back and closed her eyes. "If anyone thinks I'm weird," she mumbled, "I just don't want to hear about it."

"Did you ask me something?" a cheery voice asked. Lisa opened her eyes. Her other neighbor—the girl who'd been sitting to her right—was smiling down at her. Her dark, flashing eyes and brown curls looked vaguely familiar.

Lisa sat up. "No, I was just thinking how weird I must have looked lying down in the middle of the stage."

"Are you kidding? Everyone'll be doing that in a couple of weeks. Close to performance time Mrs. Spitz works us so hard, you can't wait for break so that you can collapse!" the girl said. "By the way, I'm Hollie. And you can look on with me after break. *I* don't mind sharing."

"I'm Lisa," Lisa said, feeling herself beginning to cheer up at Hollie's friendly greeting.

"Oh, I know," Hollie said.

"You do?" Lisa asked.

"Naturally," Hollie said. "I always prick up my ears when I hear Mrs. Spitz has found new talent."

"I'm not sure it's talent—maybe more like luck," Lisa said.

Hollie shook her head. "Nope. It's definitely talent. I heard you sing the duet with Mr. Ryan at tryouts. It was great."

Lisa smiled modestly. Then it struck her why Hollie looked familiar. "I know where I've seen you before," she said. "We read a couple of scenes together at the first audition, didn't we?"

Hollie nodded.

"I was really nervous," Lisa went on, "but you were so sure of yourself that I decided I'd fake it and just pretend I was as confident as you. You're the one who's talented."

Hollie laughed. "Hey, don't forget, that's what acting is—'faking it.' But how about if we're *both* talented?"

Lisa agreed. "So you ended up getting the head orphan part," she commented.

"Yeah, it's a good character part." At Lisa's blank look

Hollie explained. "You know, not the lead, but a part that you can do a lot with—make people remember you for other reasons than your perfect soprano. Like maybe you have a funny walk or a strange accent or just a lot of pizzazz. I get character parts a lot."

Lisa nodded, her eyes bright with enthusiasm at what Hollie was saying. She sure seemed to know a lot about the theater.

"So, you see," Hollie was finishing, "not all the orphans are as bad as Miss Sniff-sniff."

Lisa clapped her hand over her mouth to keep from laughing. "Is she usually that bad?" she asked.

"Unfortunately, yes. Anna Henchman is a completely spoiled brat. She thought she deserved the part of Annie because of her name! Can you believe that? She does have a good voice, and she's a good actress, but she makes life miserable for the rest of us. I'm sure she's jealous that you got the part. And she's probably jealous that you go riding, too. Those *are* riding clothes, aren't they?" Lisa nodded. "Well, I'm sure Anna wishes she knew how."

"Then she'd better get used to it," Lisa said, "because I go riding most days."

Hollie looked interested. "Really? That's neat. I used to ride sometimes, and I liked it," she said.

"It's the most fun thing in the world," Lisa said.

"More fun than *Annie?*" Hollie asked.

Lisa felt a pang of guilt. She didn't want to sound as though getting the lead in the play meant less to her than riding, especially when Hollie obviously cared so much about acting. "Well, just as fun," she said. Briefly she told Hollie about riding at Pine Hollow. "Why don't you come with me sometime?" she suggested.

"I'd love to," Hollie responded. "After *Annie*, that is. Of course there won't be any time before the show finishes its run."

"Um, just when will that be?" Lisa asked, trying to make her voice sound normal. It had suddenly occurred to her that there was a chance that the Pony Club rally and the play could fall on the same weekend.

Hollie seemed a bit surprised that Lisa didn't know already, but she happily filled her in on the performance dates. Dress rehearsal would be in two weeks, on a Saturday night, followed by four performances the next weekend—Friday and Saturday evenings, and Saturday and Sunday matinees.

Lisa sighed in relief. Dress rehearsal on the night of the rally would be tough, but at least it wasn't opening night. Her relief didn't last long, though. Before continuing the read-through, Mrs. Spitz handed out photocopies of the finalized rehearsal schedules. Lisa grimaced when she saw hers. As Annie, she had to be present at almost every rehearsal. There were even two rehearsals just for her alone. But that wasn't the worst part. The day of the rally she was booked from nine to eleven in the morning and seven to nine at night. What was she going to do? Ask someone else to wrap Prancer's legs, load her into the van, and get her ready for inspection in the morning, then take her home and take care of her at night? Max would never let her participate in such a halfhearted way. And she wouldn't want to. But how could she miss the rally?

"Is everything all right, Lisa?" Mrs. Spitz asked.

Lisa forced herself to nod. "Oh, yes, it's fine," she said.

Mrs. Spitz smiled sympathetically. "I know it's hard to keep up your grades when you devote yourself to a production, but I'm not worried about you, Lisa. You're a smart girl."

Lisa bit her lip. If only grades were the only thing she had to think about!

AFTER THE READ-THROUGH was over, Mrs. Spitz critiqued everyone's "performance." "Yes, it's the first rehearsal," she explained, "but when I run a show, every minute counts."

Lisa recalled hearing those words earlier that day— from Max, telling her she could get Prancer ready for the rally in time. Her head began to swim as she thought about all she had to do in the next three weeks. She hardly heard Mrs. Spitz's announcement to go downstairs to the costume room.

31

"I love this part so much!" Hollie cried, bringing Lisa back to earth.

"What part?" Lisa asked, silently reprimanding herself for not paying attention.

"You know—trying on our costumes. As soon as I see mine, I start picturing myself onstage on opening night. It makes me shiver!" Hollie hugged herself with anticipation.

Lisa followed her down the stairs and into a tiny room beneath the stage. It was crammed full of every kind of costume for every kind of show. There were racks of dresses in gingham and velvet, suit pants and jackets, farmer's overalls, lace veils, silk kimonos, and even a feather boa or two. There were rows of boots and high heels, there were piles of felt and straw hats, there were baskets of hair ribbons and sashes. In the midst of it all sat a gray-haired woman with three pins in her mouth.

"Come in, come in," she said. "I've just finished pinning up Mr. Ryan's trousers, so you can be next, Hollie."

Hollie ran and threw her arms around the woman and then introduced her to Lisa. She was Mrs. Roberts, the costume designer for more WCCT shows than anyone could remember.

While Hollie got fitted for her orphan costume, Lisa tried on the things Mrs. Roberts had given her. A little shyly, she examined herself in the full-length mirror. Her jaw dropped at the sight of herself in the red Annie dress, white tights, black patent-leather shoes, and curly red wig. With one glance all worries fled her mind.

"I'm Annie!" Lisa cried.

"AT C PICK up a working trot and circle left twenty meters," Stevie read out crisply. She and Carole had finished walking through the dressage tests that Mrs. Reg had given them and had decided to saddle up and try them on horseback before leaving for the day. Max had set up a standard "small" dressage ring—twenty by forty meters—in a flat, grassy area for them to practice in. That way they could get used to the actual size of the ring they would be riding in at the rally. Around the outside Max had placed the traditional dressage-ring letters in their proper order: A,K,E,H,C,M,B,F. The letters provided reference points for transitions from gait to gait. Stevie and Carole were taking turns reading the tests to each other.

"*E,* sitting trot, prepare to canter," Stevie continued. She looked up from the copy of the test to watch Carole and Starlight. Carole was sitting nicely in the saddle, despite the morning's workout. Starlight still looked fresh, too, but he was more relaxed, now that the first lesson had taken the edge off him. "A, canter," Stevie called. She watched Carole give the aid for the faster gait. It took a few beats past A before Starlight cantered.

"I've got to prepare him earlier." Carole panted, breaking to a trot and then a walk to talk with Stevie.

"Yup," Stevie agreed. "Maybe a couple of strides before A, you can give the aid. He looks good, though."

"Thanks, but we're nowhere near as good as you two. Dressage is just never going to be Starlight's favorite event. He's always too busy thinking about the second phase: cross-country," Carole remarked. She leaned down and patted the glossy neck. "Won't you be surprised when instead of cross-country, we do another dressage test?" she joked.

"At least Topside won't mind—he'd be content doing twenty-meter circles all day," Stevie said.

"The team is really lucky to have you two," Carole said seriously. "As Max reminded us, the lowest score wins in dressage, and I'm sure you two are his biggest hope for low marks at the rally."

Stevie nodded thoughtfully. Then she looked at Carole with a sparkle in her eye. "Finishing touches, huh?

All right, Hanson. I'll take that as a challenge. I'm going to ride the test again. This time pretend you're Max, and be as critical as possible—I mean, notice every tiny fault, okay?"

Carole was eager to agree. She dismounted and walked Starlight to the end of the ring to play judge. Stevie went through the routine. Topside walked, trotted, and cantered at exactly the right times. When she came down the center line for her final salute, Stevie was grinning. "Not too bad, huh?" she asked.

Carole consulted the piece of paper she was using to make notes on. "No, not *too* bad, although there were ten or eleven things you could work on."

"Ten or eleven things?" Stevie demanded.

Carole nodded calmly. "That's right. Like your stirrups look too short for dressage. And you didn't loosen the reins enough on the diagonal 'free walk on a loose rein.' And Topside wasn't really bending into the corners when you went counterclockwise. And you leaned down to check your canter lead—very amateurish. And he got a hair too strung out on that second canter. And I think you might have cut the circle a tiny bit short when you—"

"Okay! Okay!" Stevie cried. "I get the point. We're not perfect yet."

Carole smiled. "Not yet, but you will be soon. Now, do you want to hear the rest?"

36

Stevie listened while Carole finished reading her list of minor faults the pair had made. Then she asked Carole to watch one more time. "This time you won't be able to say a thing," she predicted confidently, trotting to the opposite end of the ring.

Unfortunately, even Topside could get his fill of dressage. He shuffled through the test like an old school horse who'd had too many lessons that day, despite Stevie's efforts to perk him up. Then Stevie started to make mistakes—very real mistakes—in addition to the minor errors Carole had noted. About halfway through, after Stevie had been rising to the wrong diagonal for about ten beats, Carole called out for her to stop.

"I don't remember there being a halt here," Stevie said, when she had coaxed the now fussy Topside to stand still.

"You're right—there is no halt," Carole replied. "But it's about time we both *called* a halt to practicing for today. I hate to say it, but my list of problems for this test is already longer than for the last one, and you're only halfway through."

"I know," Stevie acknowledged. "I could feel Topside getting fed up with doing the same stuff again. I guess I got a little overenthusiastic, huh?" she asked. She had loosened the reins and was letting Topside walk freely. The bay gelding blew through his nostrils as if heaving a sigh.

"We both did," Carole said. "Look—it's almost dusk. We've been here all day. And I know Max wouldn't want us going crazy this early on in the game, so let's head in."

Stevie agreed. She hopped off Topside and gave him a good, long pat. "I guess it's just that when you have horses as great as Topside and Starlight, it makes you want to ride forever," she said, grinning.

"Right," Carole said, "and so does having a trainer who works you as hard as Max."

They were silent as they led the horses toward the barn. Finally Stevie put both of their thoughts into words. "I wish Lisa could have been here to practice, too. Prancer's greener than Starlight, and flightier, too. Squeezing in practice time might not cut it if she doesn't settle down and—"

Before she could finish, she was interrupted by Lisa running toward them. Her face was easy to make out, even in the near dusk, because it was covered in base makeup, powder, eye shadow, and lipstick. "Hey, you guys!" she called.

Carole and Stevie looked at one another. There couldn't have been a worse time for Lisa to arrive. Both of them were totally spent.

"Phew! I was so afraid I'd miss you, but we ended up getting out ten minutes early, and I came right over after

38

we tried on our costumes and makeup. I didn't even take off any of my paint!" Lisa smiled happily.

"Umm . . . ," Carole began cautiously. "Listen, Lisa, Stevie and I are going in now. We've each gone through our tests a few times, we're exhausted, and Starlight and Topside are bored. It wouldn't be fair to them or us to keep practicing."

Lisa looked crestfallen. "I'm tired, too, but I'm willing to keep on working. Besides, it'll only take fifteen minutes for me to get Prancer ready, and twenty minutes to ride."

Stevie decided to be practical. "Where are you going to ride, anyway? It's almost too dark out here, and the indoor ring is taken up by an adult lesson."

"And, anyway, they'll be feeding Prancer in a half hour. Even if you could get tacked up in five minutes, she wouldn't be any fun to ride now, because she'd be so cranky for her dinner," Carole pointed out.

"I'm feeling kind of cranky myself," Stevie chimed in, trying to make light of the situation.

Lisa didn't smile. "I guess that extra ten minutes is just going to go to waste then," she said sulkily. She could hardly believe Carole and Stevie weren't going to make an effort to practice with her after she'd made a huge effort to get all the way back to Pine Hollow after a long rehearsal.

"Ten minutes, huh?" Stevie asked. Lisa nodded.

"Well," Stevie continued, "if you've got ten extra minutes, how about we spend them together at TD's? I know I could use an ice-cream sundae or two."

"Sounds good," Carole said. "We haven't had any quality Saddle Club time in a while."

Lisa thought for a minute and then shook her head. With a schedule like hers, spending time at the local ice-cream shop seemed like *wasting* time—something she couldn't afford to do. She'd already wasted enough time coming over to Pine Hollow in the first place. The only thing to do now was to get her script and leave. "I don't think I can go. I'm going to have to look at my time schedule again, and I need my computer for that." She turned on her heel as they reached the barn doors. "See you at class Tuesday," she added briskly. With that she hurried into the tack room to call for a ride, leaving Carole and Lisa to walk, groom, and feed the horses.

A few minutes later they saw her walking to the end of the driveway to meet her mother. Her script was open, and she was trying to read it in the diminishing light.

"Hey, I forgot to ask—how was the rehearsal?" Carole called. Lisa was already out of earshot and did not respond.

"I forgot to ask, too," Stevie said quietly.

A gloom hung over them as they untacked and

brushed Topside and Starlight on opposite cross-ties. Neither of them talked much.

On their way out they spotted Prancer in her stall. She was munching hay. As usual, though, she wasn't simply plowing through her two leaves of timothy and alfalfa. Instead she took a few bites and then looked up over her stall door to make sure she wasn't missing anything. She pricked up her ears at any noise, and occasionally she would try to reach her nose into the stalls on either side of hers to get her neighbors' attention before going back to her hay. She wasn't doing anything wrong. And it wasn't that she was really nervous. But she was young and a Thoroughbred and had come to Pine Hollow straight from the track—and it showed.

Carole and Stevie watched her for a few minutes, taking in her high-strung behavior. Neither of them said anything, but they were both thinking the same thing: Of all of the Horse Wise mounts, Prancer needed the most practice time.

5

LISA DRUMMED HER fingers on the computer keyboard in frustration. Here it was, almost time for dinner, and instead of memorizing the lines to her first scene, she was still trying to perfect her schedule. Try as she did, she couldn't squeeze everything in. And she was already planning to do homework on the morning and afternoon buses.

"Twenty-four hours is too short for a whole day!" she cried. By Lisa's calculations she needed about twenty-nine. It had been bad enough giving up free time at Pine Hollow for rehearsals, and that was before Max had even announced the news about dressage rally. Even if she never helped out or cleaned her tack once, she wouldn't be able to find enough time for riding. And by the looks on their faces when she had left, Stevie and Carole weren't too excited about her taking off without pitching in.

Reluctantly she began typing her rehearsal times onto the screen again. Every time she saw an afternoon time slot fill up, she cringed. She knew that both of the things Max had said were true: Prancer *was* a lot better than before, but she still had a long way to go to be ready for a Pony Club rally.

The phone rang three times before Lisa unwillingly picked it up. How would she explain that she couldn't talk to Stevie or Carole right now when they had been nice enough to call?

"Hello?" she said uncertainly.

To her surprise neither Stevie nor Carole answered. Instead a cheery, low-toned voice asked, " 'Hello?' Is that all ya got to say to a feller orphan?"

"Hollie?" Lisa asked.

"That's right—guess I couldn't fool you," Hollie kidded. "Anyway, I just called up to talk shop—see what you thought of the cast, you know."

Lisa settled back in her chair, suddenly glad for the interruption. "I like everyone but Anna Henchman," she answered truthfully. "What do you think?"

"Same," Hollie replied. "So you're happy you tried out?"

"Definitely," Lisa answered. "Are you?"

"Oh, I'm incredibly happy," Hollie replied. "I'm always in a good mood as soon as I start working on a new show. Heck, I'd be a sword carrier if I had to. And I think musicals are much more fun than straight drama."

"A sword carrier?" Lisa repeated. "I didn't know there were any of those in *Annie*."

"Oh, that's just what you call people with tiny, non-speaking parts, no matter what the play," Hollie explained.

"You've done a lot of plays, haven't you?" Lisa asked. She loved listening to Hollie talk "theater-speak." She felt the way she had when she started riding, and heard words like "tack," "dressage," and "palomino" for the first times.

"More than I can count," Hollie answered. "I started as an angel in our church Christmas pageant when I was three, and I've been acting on and off—but mostly on—since then. I just love it."

"Do you ever think about trying to become a professional actress?" Lisa asked.

"Only about twenty-two hours a day," Hollie admitted, laughing.

"What about the other two hours?" Lisa teased.

"The other two hours I'm rehearsing, so I can't think about it."

The two girls laughed. Lisa was thrilled to be hitting it off with an experienced member of the cast. She was even more excited to be making a new friend with such an interesting hobby. She listened, fascinated, as Hollie told her one funny tale after another about plays she'd been in. Even though Hollie made light of her achievement, it was obvious that she was a serious actress already. She took voice, dance, and diction lessons on the side to round out her acting ability. She had seen a few Broadway shows in New York and had even been backstage once, to visit a cast member who was a family friend.

"I had a part in a movie once, you know," Lisa put in playfully.

"You *did?*" Hollie asked.

"Yup. My friends and I were in a movie with Skye Ransom," she said. Hollie squealed so loudly Lisa had to hold the phone away from her ear.

"What? Did you say what I think you said? You were in a *movie* and with *Skye Ransom?*" Hollie cried.

Lisa giggled at Hollie's reaction. The whole thing had happened in such a funny way that she and Stevie and Carole tended to forget what a big deal it was. Briefly she related the story of The Saddle Club's trip to New York for the American Horse Show, Skye Ransom's problems riding, their helping him out, and the subsequent movie appearance.

"Oh, my gosh," Hollie said reverently. "I saw that one about five times. I even remember your scene. Yes, I do

45

—I'm positive—I remember the riding scene with the three girls because I remember thinking that they looked about my age. And you weren't just *in* it, you *know* him —I mean, you're *friends* with him." Hollie paused to sigh. "Wow, that's one of the coolest things I've ever heard. And here *I* was going to try to encourage *you* to think about professional acting. You should be the one convincing me!"

"Professional acting? Are you kidding?" Lisa appreciated Hollie's compliment, but she could no sooner imagine devoting herself to the stage than she could imagine running off to join the circus. She said as much to Hollie.

"Maybe you don't think so now, but you're really talented, and when people find out, you're going to have to act in a lot of plays—just to appease your fans," Hollie said.

"You really think I'm talented?" Lisa blurted out.

"I really do, Lisa. Look, you've got stage presence, a good voice, a natural sense of timing, and you're pretty, too. Not a bad start for an actress, dear," Hollie said, putting on a funny, old-lady voice.

Lisa didn't know how to thank Hollie enough for boosting her confidence. All day she had been doubting herself—in acting and riding—and Hollie's words had made her feel a hundred times better.

The two girls talked awhile longer. Hollie filled her in

on all the WCCT gossip—who had been in what plays, whom Mrs. Spitz liked best in the chorus, what big cities Mr. Ryan had toured in his prime as an actor. The only problem with talking to Hollie was that Lisa felt a tiny bit fake. Yes, she was enthusiastic about the play, but she could hardly imagine being as single-minded as Hollie. She kept wanting to mention The Saddle Club and Prancer, but somehow she knew Hollie wouldn't understand her conflict any better than Carole and Stevie did. They loved riding; Hollie loved acting. Lisa didn't know exactly where she fit in.

Before long Mrs. Atwood called Lisa to come to dinner. Lisa glanced at her watch and grimaced. Six-thirty! She was supposed to have completed her schedule and her reading homework before dinner. So much for that. Lisa reluctantly told Hollie she had to hang up for dinner.

"Okay, Annie, see you tomorrow. It should be a fun rehearsal because we're going to start blocking," Hollie predicted.

"What's blocking?" Lisa asked.

"Blocking? No one told you? That's when you plan out the action of the play with the director. Mrs. Spitz tells you where to stand when you give your lines, where to enter and exit, all that. It's fun because you really begin to see how the play is going to look," Hollie explained.

47

"It does sound fun," Lisa admitted. It was obvious that there were a lot of words and other things about the theater that she was still going to have to learn. On an inspiration she suggested, "Hey, maybe you can be my stage coach, Hollie, and help me understand the acting world."

"I'm happy to help you with anything," Hollie replied warmly. Then she commented, "Hey, you know, that's funny—even when you're talking about acting, you use riding words."

"What do you mean?" Lisa asked.

"You just said I'd be your *stage coach*—you know, like a horse and carriage, right?" Hollie asked.

"Yeah, that is funny," Lisa agreed, but she didn't feel like laughing. She had missed the pun entirely, and for some reason it made her uneasy that Hollie knew she thought about horses a lot of the time, even though it was true.

"Anyway, don't let mean old Mrs. Hannigan get to you tonight," Hollie kidded.

Lisa smiled into the receiver. "Don't worry, I'll keep an eye out," she promised.

After hanging up she took another glance at her schedule. It looked just as impossible as before. The worst part was that somehow she was going to have to explain her lack of free time, Pine Hollow time, riding time, and Saddle Club time to Stevie and Carole.

Lisa sighed. At the back of her mind she had known it would be hard to make them understand. Carole was totally devoted to riding and horses. She wanted to be a professional rider and trainer, an equine vet, a steeple-chase jockey, an instructor, or any one of a dozen things that meant dedicating her life to horses. Stevie didn't talk as seriously about her favorite activity as Carole did, but she basically loved two things: horses and having fun.

Lisa had discovered riding later than her two friends. She had the kind of mother who believed girls should be well-rounded. Mrs. Atwood had enrolled her daughter in every kind of after-school activity, from ballet and music to Girl Scouts—and finally to riding. The minute she'd started taking lessons at Pine Hollow, Lisa had known that she liked riding better than almost anything she'd tried. She'd worked hard and caught up fast. But there was a part of her that occasionally missed stuff like piano and tap dancing. When she'd seen the poster at the mall advertising *Annie* auditions, Lisa had decided on her own, without any urging from her mother, that she wanted to try out. As it turned out, all the after-school music and dance lessons had paid off at the auditions. What was more, Lisa had discovered something else: She had stage presence. She loved being up on the stage, and it showed. How was she supposed to explain all that to Stevie and Carole?

As she stared at the afternoon block on the computer screen, her mother's voice calling "Dinner, Lisa!" floated up to her again. Reluctantly Lisa stood. She usually enjoyed taking a break from homework to eat with the family. But for the next few weeks, dinner was going to mean one thing and one thing only: that the afternoon was all used up.

CAROLE AND STEVIE stood in the doorway of TD's. Normally, they would have slid right into their usual booth, but somehow it didn't seem right to sit there without Lisa. They found themselves choosing a table for two in the middle of the ice-cream parlor.

"Barely recognized you guys, sitting over here," the waitress remarked when she came to take the order. "Where's the third musketeer?"

"If you must know, she couldn't make it today," Stevie said, sounding more touchy than she meant to.

"Easy does it, honey. You can come here just the two of you. I was only asking. Now, what'll it be? Mustard ice cream with ketchup sauce?" The waitress chuckled at her own joke. She was used to Stevie's bizarre flavor and topping combinations, and every once in a while she liked to try to one-up her.

Stevie gave her a withering glance. "Good idea," she said sarcastically, "but I'm too upset to eat. How about a nice, plain old butterscotch sundae—on pistachio."

The waitress shrugged. "You call that 'nice' and 'plain'? That's a good one," she muttered.

Carole didn't feel much like eating either. Finally she decided, "I'll have whatever you recommend."

The waitress couldn't have looked more surprised if Stevie had ordered vanilla with hot fudge. "You've been coming here since you were little kids, and now you want me to recommend something?"

Carole nodded gravely. "I just can't decide today."

"Jeez, whatever's eating you two is pretty bad. I'll bring you a nice chocolate shake. That'll make you feel better." Shaking her head, the waitress went to the counter to fix their orders.

When she left, Carole and Stevie slouched back in their chairs. "I think *Annie* really means a lot to Lisa," Carole said after a few minutes. She had been trying to think of other topics of conversation, but for once she could think of only one thing to talk about with Stevie. Everything else seemed unimportant.

Stevie nodded. "She even had her makeup on when she came to ride."

"She really ran to make it back, didn't she?" Carole asked.

"I guess she'll be running a lot from now on with that schedule."

"No doubt—you saw how fast she took off."

"Carole, are you worried, too?" Stevie asked.

51

Carole looked up. "You mean about today?"

"About today, tomorrow, the next three weeks—and after," Stevie said. "For all we know, Lisa might find out she likes acting better than riding and—"

"And decide to quit Horse Wise, Pine Hollow, and The Saddle Club altogether so she can devote her life to the stage," Carole finished for her.

"She can't keep up this schedule forever. That's for sure," Stevie murmured as the waitress set down their orders.

"Enjoy," the woman said, looking at Carole, "and *try* to enjoy, if it's humanly possible," she told Stevie.

Carole mechanically took a couple bites of ice cream. She didn't notice whose dish she was eating out of until Stevie grabbed it defensively. "Hey! Hands off my concoction. If you want something this good, you've got to order it, Hanson."

Carole snapped to attention, turning her mouth down as the pistachio-butterscotch combination hit her. "Ugh, I was so busy thinking about Lisa, I forgot to think about my taste buds." She grabbed her milk shake to wash it down, but after a few sips she pushed the glass aside. "It's no use. This hardly tastes any better. She could serve me strawberry shortcake, and I wouldn't feel like eating it."

Stevie spooned her sundae pensively. "You know what our problem is? We're not treating this like a normal problem. What do we always do to solve normal problems?"

"Make them Saddle Club projects," Carole answered promptly.

"Exactly," Stevie said.

"But this isn't a Saddle Club project. The Saddle Club's the *problem*. I mean, the problem is with The Saddle Club project. I mean—oh, you know what I mean," Carole finished, exasperated.

"What you're trying to say is that The Saddle Club's problem is The Saddle Club problem, and therefore, there's no reason why The Saddle Club can't solve it— even if that means the two of us," Stevie announced. She was actually beginning to sound cheerful about the situation. "Right?"

Carole looked unconvinced. "I guess so, but what are you suggesting?"

"It's easy. Lisa is on the brink of making a huge mistake: abandoning the two most important things in her life—riding and us, her best friends. Unless someone helps her now, she could regret this for years. She needs help—and fast. We'll provide it. We'll be there for her at all times. Starting with Tuesday, no matter how tired we are, we'll stay after class, practice with her, coach her, give her advice. It's not as if we have to go running off after the lesson ends, so we'll just make the decision to stay. We won't do barn chores until after she leaves. If

53

my straight-A average suffers a little, I'll just have to be satisfied with B-pluses." Stevie grinned impishly. Although she was known for many things, perfect grades wasn't one of them. In fact, she probably would have loved perfect B-pluses!

Carole found herself smiling, too, in spite of herself. Stevie's enthusiasm was infectious. She made it sound so simple. There was no way Lisa would quit riding if they totally supported her for the next few weeks. "Okay, Stevie, I'm in," she said.

With that the two girls clinked water glasses. They were about to embark on a new Saddle Club project— maybe the most serious one they'd ever attempted.

"HAT, GLOVES, BOOTS, saddle, bridle," Lisa said aloud. She was giving herself and Prancer a quick once-over before joining the Tuesday-afternoon lesson, which had started five minutes ago.

The end of the previous week and the weekend had flown by, and lately she'd been so scattered that it honestly wouldn't have surprised her to find out that she'd forgotten to put on a piece of tack. She'd already been chastised by Max for her late arrival. She didn't want to upset him further by showing up unprepared. Besides, she had a feeling that she ought to stay on Max's good side as much as possible or risk a lecture sometime soon. No doubt he had noticed her absence from the stable over the weekend and wasn't particularly pleased.

"Red, do we look okay?" she asked.

Pine Hollow's chief stable hand looked up from the grain he was mixing for the evening feeding. He surveyed the pair critically. "You look fine except for one thing."

"What?" Lisa demanded anxiously.

"You look about as happy as a horse with a twitch on her nose."

Lisa let out a deep sigh. Red was right. She had also been discovering lately how hard it was to enjoy things that you barely had time for. The truth was, she *wasn't* really looking forward to the lesson, because she hadn't ridden—and more important, hadn't ridden Prancer—in three days. She was nervous about how the mare would perform in front of the others and whether she'd be able to control her.

She gave Red a grin. "Is that better?"

"A little. But it would be even better if you meant it."

Lisa sighed again. "I know. You're right," she said.

"Now, you go in there and enjoy yourself. What's a young girl like you got to worry about anyway, huh?"

"Nothing, Red—absolutely nothing," Lisa said. She turned and hurried into the indoor ring, not wanting to talk anymore. She was also getting used to pretending everything was fine. If she let down her guard in front of Red, Max, her mother, Hollie, Mrs. Spitz—even Stevie and Carole—they would just tell her to quit either the play or the rally. And she was *not* going to quit either one. No matter what. Setting her jaw determinedly, Lisa mounted and trotted over to join the others.

Max was setting up a grid of cavalletti at various heights with varying distances in between them. "We're doing grids today, Lisa, as soon as everyone's warmed up. Walk, trot, and canter on your own while I finish setting up," he instructed.

Lisa was puzzled. She had assumed they would be riding only on the flat like before in order to prepare for the rally. "Shouldn't we be doing dressage today?" she asked.

Max looked up from the jumps. "If you'd been here at the start of class, Lisa, you'd have heard me explain that we don't want the horses to get bored or sour. To keep them fresh and interested in flat work, we're going to continue to jump in lessons. And I've advised everyone to take trail rides as well as schooling on our off days. This particular cavalletti exercise can be very relaxing for both the horse and the rider. It should take the edge off some of these superfit horses—such as Prancer—and perk up the lazier ones so they'll all work better later."

Wordlessly, Lisa absorbed what Max was saying. She was left with one question, and she hardly dared ask it. She took a deep breath. "Uh—later?" she repeated in a barely audible voice.

"Right. We're going to take a break at four-thirty, go

over some rules questions, and have a short, intensive flat session at five."

Lisa was about to explain that she had to be at rehearsal at quarter after five when she suddenly lost her nerve. She glanced at Max. She had never been truly afraid to tell him something before, no matter how strict she knew he might be. But what could he say if she told him about rehearsal? It was practically the same as saying "Acting means more to me than riding." In her mind Lisa knew the response: "No, it doesn't. It's just that I got a starring role my first time out, I seem to be good at it, and I like it." But then she heard Max saying, "How can you be sure acting won't always come first?"

"Because it won't," Lisa murmured to herself. "Just please let me do both. I know I can—really, I can."

At the sound of Max clapping his hands, Lisa shook the confused thoughts from her mind. Prancer had already shied at imaginary ghosts twice, and Lisa had had to quiet her. The important thing now was warming up quickly and riding for as long and as well as she could.

To Lisa's surprise Prancer behaved far better for the rest of the lesson. As soon as they began jumping through the grid, the mare seemed to settle down to business. Max's comments of "Nice!" and "Good job!" made Lisa glow from head to foot.

Everyone looked happy and relaxed as they jumped

the cavalletti, first without stirrups, then without stirrups or reins—their arms crossed on their chests—and finally, without stirrups or reins and with their eyes closed. "Whoo-eee!" Stevie hollered after going through the last time. She grabbed the knotted reins from Topside's neck and asked him to slow to a trot. "It felt like Topside was taking off for the sky," she said.

"It is a great feeling, isn't it?" Max asked, summoning them all to the center. "Why do you think so?"

Carole raised her hand. "You really feel together with your horse. You feel totally balanced, and so does he. And there's a perfect rhythm because of the spacing between the cavalletti: five bounces in a row."

Max nodded vigorously. "Exactly. You got what I was hinting at, and that's rhythm. Rhythm is always important in riding. You've got to establish a good, working rhythm on the flat and learn to keep it over fences. The spacing of the jumps, as you said, Carole, forced them to jump in an even rhythm. That's what I want you to keep in mind most today as you ride your tests. I want to be able to set a metronome to Topside's trot, Stevie. And Lisa, I want Prancer's canter to make me think of a Beethoven sonata. All right, everyone take ten minutes for a water break, and be back at five. Sharp."

Lisa stared numbly at Max. She had gotten so caught up in riding Prancer that she had forgotten about rehearsal. The big clock on the wall read five minutes to five. Lisa would just have time to untack, give Prancer a quick grooming, and fly. For a second she let herself think of lingering at Pine Hollow, eating ice cream at TD's, and heading home for a relaxed family dinner. It seemed like forever since she'd been able just to hang out, but it had actually been less than a week.

Gritting her teeth, she swung off the big mare and gave her a pat. "Thank you for being so good even though I haven't ridden you," Lisa whispered in her ear.

"Keep up the good work, Lisa," Max said as he dragged the cavalletti to the side of the ring. Lisa nodded silently. She still couldn't say anything. She just couldn't.

"COME ON, YOU two—let's talk, 'Enter working trot sitting' back in the indoor ring," Carole called. She led Starlight toward the ring, beckoning for Lisa and Stevie to follow. The three of them had watered their horses and grabbed a quick drink for themselves before regrouping for the flat session. Or at least Carole and Stevie had. Unknown to them, however, Lisa had untacked Prancer and put her away for the evening.

"Ready?" Stevie asked.

Lisa bit her lip. "Stevie," she began, "I know this is kind of a big request, but could you tell Max that I, uh, can't make the five o'clock flat lesson?"

Stevie looked puzzled. "Sure, Lisa. But don't you want to tell him yourself?"

Lisa shook her head. "I would, but I can't. I've really got to run. Rehearsal starts at quarter after five, and I told my mom to get here five minutes ago. She's going to drive me over. I don't want to explain to Max about— you know."

Stevie put a reassuring arm around Lisa's shoulders. "I do know, and listen, don't worry. I'll tell Max that you're going to ride later. Carole and I can meet you back here at seven. Prancer will have eaten by then, and she'll be all ready for an evening schooling session with The Saddle Club."

Lisa looked surprised. "Oh, I can't come *back*, Stevie," she said. "I've got a history essay due tomorrow, and I'm one assignment behind in math—which even if I do in the morning on the bus, I'll only get halfway through— and I've got to memorize all my lines by evening rehearsal. It's not as if I'm an apple seller with two words to say. Annie is a huge part—the biggest. There are pages and pages of cues and blocking to learn, too, in addition to the actual lines. Hollie's been studying her part every night. But thanks for telling Max. 'Bye!"

As she spoke, Lisa had begun to edge away. When she called her good-bye, she was through the door and running up the driveway as fast as she could. Stevie stared after her. Cues? Blocking? *Hollie?* Was this the new Lisa with new words and new friends? Stevie frowned. If so, she didn't like the new Lisa. The old one would have faced Max and told him about her rehearsal. But then, Stevie thought, the old Lisa wouldn't have had a rehearsal to tell him about. She sighed and went to get Topside.

Five minutes later, when she told Max the news, he raised his eyebrows but said nothing about Lisa and Prancer. Instead he told Stevie to pick up a trot and quit slouching. Stevie was relieved. She would much rather have Max correct her position than get angry at Lisa. On the other hand, she didn't necessarily think that his silence was a good thing. It probably meant that he was brooding and that Lisa would hear about it later.

The rest of the lesson went well. Rather than go through all their dressage tests from start to finish, Max had them select the parts they thought were the most difficult. He worked with them all individually. Betsy was enjoying riding Barq but had trouble keeping her canter circles small enough. Carole couldn't get Starlight to bend around the corners. Veronica and Polly wanted to work on their entrances and exits. Finally Stevie was the only one left.

"All right, Stevie, how about it?" Max asked.

Stevie had been thinking as hard as she could while Max coached the others, but she had come up empty. Topside just didn't have one problem area. "I couldn't think of anything Topside was bad at," she said, steeling herself for the worst. Max always said it was the rider's fault if he or she didn't know what to practice. It also sounded a lot like something Veronica would say. To her surprise Max simply asked her to show him what she'd been working on. Happily, she put Topside through his paces, throwing in a few circles, two halts, and even some leg yielding on the diagonal. Max nodded knowingly. "Just as I suspected," he said. "You're completely right."

"I *am?*" Stevie asked incredulously.

"Yup. Topside has never looked better."

Stevie sat up straighter in the saddle and smiled. "Why, thank you, I—" she began.

"But you, my dear, could use some work," Max finished.

The class burst out laughing at the shocked expression on Stevie's face. "Me?" she asked.

"You," Max said succinctly. The class tittered. "Seriously, Stevie, do you understand what I mean?"

Stevie thought for a minute. "I think so. You're saying that Topside is doing everything perfectly even though I'm not always *telling* him to do everything perfectly."

"Precisely." Max turned to the rest of the class. "That's an important lesson to learn. You're all going to have a perfectly schooled horse someday, just like Topside—a good mover, an old hand at dressage—and he's going to make you look great. But you have to live up to your horse. You can't just, ahem, *slouch* along for the ride like a sack of potatoes. In many ways you're lucky with a horse like Topside. You don't have to worry so much about his behavior, so you can work doubly hard on your own skills. Got it, Stevie?"

"Got it," Stevie said. Then she leaned over his neck and in a loud stage whisper, added, "Don't worry, boy. As of right now, this sack of potatoes is turning back into a girl."

Everyone laughed again until Max called an end to the lesson. On their way in Carole and Stevie were too caught up in discussing what the two of them *had* learned in the lesson to remember to worry about what Lisa hadn't.

LISA PUT DOWN her pen with a flourish. "History paper, done," she said aloud. How good the paper was, she couldn't be sure. "At least it's done," she told herself.

The digital clock by Lisa's bed read 9:09. Unbelievably, she was right on schedule—actually, three minutes ahead of time. She even had a five-minute break scheduled between "Write paper" and "Memorize Lines." That meant eight whole minutes of free time. Without another thought she dialed Stevie, who conference-called Carole.

The first thing Lisa wanted to hear about was what she had missed in the dressage lesson. Carole and Stevie described the class to her, including Max's advice to Stevie and Stevie's reply.

"A sack of potatoes?" Lisa demanded. "You've never looked like a sack of potatoes in your life!"

"I know! Maybe a sack of carrots or a sack of onions or even a sack of flour—but potatoes? Really!" Stevie said haughtily.

"To Max, hunching your shoulders for two beats translates as looking like a sack of potatoes," Carole commented dryly.

Lisa asked how Starlight had done. Carole said she was pleased. "I really think he's improving every day. Today was perfect for him because we'd already jumped, so he was a lot quieter on the flat. He's still not bending around the corners, but at least he seems to be listening."

"I wish I could have been there," Lisa said. "Prancer and I really could have used that individual attention."

Tactfully Carole changed the subject to Lisa's rehearsal. Lisa obviously felt bad enough about not riding in the second lesson without their going on and on about it.

"You really want to know?" Lisa asked.

"Of course! We just haven't seen you very much, so we haven't had the chance to ask you," Carole said.

Naturally, Lisa couldn't wait to tell them about being in the play. She had saved up stories about the different actors and the funny mistakes people made—like the time Mr. Ryan had come onstage at the wrong time.

Instead of stopping the rehearsal, he had said, "Oh, dear, I seem to be in the wrong scene. Won't you excuse me?" and walked offstage, still in character.

When she had finished, Stevie said, "It sounds great, Lisa." She really meant it, too. Before, she had thought actors all took themselves very seriously. From what Lisa said, though, there was at least as much clowning around at *Annie* as there was at Pine Hollow.

"It is great. It really is. It's just—" Lisa stopped mid-sentence. In the middle of talking her voice had choked up.

"What?" Carole asked. "What's wrong?"

Lisa gulped. She went on, her voice quavering. "It's just that everyone else is ten times more experienced than I am, and I have to ask stupid questions every two seconds. It's so embarrassing. Hollie—this girl who's a great actress and really nice, too—she's been helping me. But I feel like a total ignoramus! I didn't know what 'blocking' was, or 'downstage' or 'stage right' or anything. And everyone else knows. It's not like the school plays, where there are always a bunch of little kids in the chorus. WCCT is really serious. I feel like I'm out of my league."

"But even though they're really experienced, you're the one who got the lead, Lisa. You can't forget that," Carole said.

"I guess so," Lisa said glumly. "Sometimes that makes

it worse, though. I have the feeling that they think I don't deserve the lead."

"Who's 'they'?" Carole asked. "The director? She cast you as Annie. Mr. Ryan? You said he told you you had a great voice. Hollie? She sounds really friendly."

"Oh, she *is*," Lisa said. "I know you both would like her. She's as crazy about acting as you—I mean, we—are about riding. But I still wish there were a production just for idiots. This afternoon I had to ask what 'off book' meant."

"Well, what does it mean?" Carole asked.

"Just what it sounds like: It means you don't need to use your script anymore. We're supposed to be 'off book' by tomorrow, or the end of the week at the latest. Of course I had to interrupt Mrs. Spitz to ask that."

"Everybody has to interrupt the director to learn that stuff when they get their first part. If I started to act, I wouldn't know," Stevie pointed out.

"That's right, they should be sympathetic," Carole added.

Lisa had to admit that most of the cast was helpful and nice to her. "I guess I'm letting one girl get to me too much," she said. She told them about Anna, the girl who didn't like the smell of horses. Since that first incident she had continued to be rude to Lisa, laughing when Lisa asked a question and whispering behind her back.

"Sounds like she's the Veronica diAngelo of the play," Stevie said.

In spite of herself Lisa started to giggle. Stevie had really hit the nail on the head. Anna *was* the Veronica of the play. She was stuck-up, she was spoiled, and she was mean. Somehow, comparing the two girls helped put things in perspective. After all, Lisa had always been able to handle Veronica, so why should she let this other rude girl get the better of her?

"Too bad we're not in the play, or we could really make things hard for this Anna character," Stevie said, doing her best to imitate a gangster in an old movie.

"I'll just have to rely on Hollie's and my ability to get even," Lisa said. "She's my stage coach, you know." Lisa explained what the term meant and how Hollie had noticed that Lisa used horsey words even to describe things that were totally unrelated to horses.

"That's the spirit, Lisa. You've got to wake these actors up to a whole new world outside of stage right and stage left. Maybe they'll learn something, too," Stevie said enthusiastically.

"Exactly," Carole added. "Who knows—in some way Hollie might learn as much from you as you do from her. It's like when you and May Grover teamed up."

Lisa had to laugh. Carole was referring to Lisa's partnership with May Grover, a younger rider at Pine Hollow. Supposedly Lisa had been teaching May how to harness a pony to a cart. Instead, May had taught Lisa everything.

"One thing's for sure," Lisa said, "I'd like to teach Anna Henchman a thing or two!" She was surprised to hear herself joking around. Then again, she thought, with Stevie and Carole it was impossible not to. Of course the eight minutes had long since passed. Lisa didn't mind, though. She always got more work done when she was in a good mood. She did have to go, however. Reluctantly she got ready to say her good-byes.

"Time to memorize, huh?" Stevie asked.

"You got it," Lisa said. Before hanging up she thanked Stevie and Carole for all their support and apologized for all the time she hadn't spent with them. And there was one more order of business to take care of. If they were going to be at Pine Hollow, Lisa wanted them to assure Max that she was doing everything she could to spend all the time possible at the stable. "Could you tell him I'm working with Prancer as much as I can?" she asked. "I'm absolutely, positively going to be there for the rally —although I might have to leave just a tad early—and I promise, cross my heart, to do everything I have to so Prancer will be completely ready in two—I mean one and a half—weeks," Lisa finished breathlessly.

Stevie and Carole knew that Max would respond better if Lisa's pledge came from Lisa, not from them. They didn't want to add another worry to her list, though.

Both girls promised to do all they could to persuade Max that Prancer would be ready.

After Lisa hung up, Stevie wasted no time in summing up the situation. "Well, she hasn't forgotten about us yet," she said.

"No, she hasn't. And we're not going to forget about her, either. We'll smooth things over with Max about practice," Carole vowed.

"Even if everything's okay with him, though, it's going to be tough for Lisa to get Prancer ready. I think the worst thing would be for her to go and really mess up, like she did at the last show with Prancer," said Stevie.

Carole agreed. "I might want to quit riding after two horrible shows," she speculated.

"I can hardly see you wanting to quit, Carole Hanson," Stevie remarked.

"You're right," Carole wailed. "I don't have anything else to do!"

Stevie burst out laughing. She knew exactly what Carole meant, but it sounded hilarious. Both she and Carole were completely happy riding, doing Horse Wise, seeing their boyfriends, Phil and Cam, when they could, and—for Stevie's part—getting in and out of trouble. They liked to think of school as something they did on the side.

Lisa was different. She cared a lot about grades, and

judging from her success at the auditions, she was a talented actress.

"I understand what you're saying," Stevie said when she had controlled her chuckles. "We're both afraid that being great at two things—four if you count acting, singing, and dancing, all of which she has to do in the play—is going to force Lisa to choose."

"And she might not choose riding," Carole finished. "Especially if she thinks she's not doing a good job."

"You know what I say? Saddle Club meeting at Pine Hollow tomorrow afternoon," Stevie decided.

"Without Lisa?" Carole asked. She didn't want them to get too used to having two-person meetings.

"Lisa will be there in spirit, because that's what we're going to talk about," Stevie answered, "Getting her to this rally and keeping her in The Saddle Club. If we don't have the meeting, her days being there for real might be numbered."

Carole had to agree.

WHEN CAROLE GOT to Pine Hollow the next day, she was all set to sit down with Stevie and plan their attack. She had spent her English and math classes jotting down points they could use to persuade Lisa to put acting second—at least once the play had ended. Stevie, however, seemed to have already made—and activated—her own plan. She was saddled up and riding outside. She waved to Carole from the outdoor ring. Carole waved back automatically and then stopped in her tracks. Instead of Topside Stevie was riding Prancer.

Suddenly it hit Carole. Why hadn't they thought of that before? Prancer needed work, and so did Stevie. Topside, on the other hand, did not. The most important thing was keeping him fresh and interested for the rally. A little light schooling and a trail ride or two would do the trick. Riding Prancer, Stevie could sharpen her skills *and* help Lisa get the mare ready.

"Pretty good idea, huh?" Stevie called, trotting down the long side of the ring.

"Are you kidding? It's a *great* idea!" Carole yelled after her. She watched the mare's briskly swinging trot for a few minutes in admiration. She looked energetic but relaxed. Stevie sat proudly in the saddle. At the end of the ring they picked up a canter. Prancer chucked the bit up in her teeth and shied away from the rail. Stevie laughed and made her trot until she stopped playing. They were obviously enjoying each other immensely.

"Want someone to watch you?" Carole asked when Stevie approached again.

"Definitely—we can use all the constructive criticism we can get." She brought Prancer down to a walk and came over to Carole for a quick chat.

"I'll be your 'stage coach' first, as Lisa said, and then we can switch," Carole commented.

"It's a deal," Stevie said.

For the next half hour the two girls gave Prancer an intensive private lesson. Carole planted herself in the middle of the ring and barked criticism and commands. "Too fast! Too late! Canter now!" Far from being an annoying chore, watching and coaching was more fun than Carole could have imagined. As she critiqued

Stevie and Prancer, she found herself thinking how high-spirited and eager Prancer was. She was sleek, fast, and feisty and could be difficult.

Funny, Carole mused, that sounded a lot like Stevie. In the long run, the mare would probably do better with someone who was steady, organized, and methodical—someone like Lisa. For now, though, both she and Stevie would benefit from the partnership.

Carole had them walk, trot, halt, walk, trot, canter, trot, halt, trot, walk, trot, canter until Stevie was breathing hard and Prancer was sweating even in the brisk fall air. Then she put them through circles, figure eights, leg yielding, center lines, and more circles. As they worked, the girls compared their impressions of how Prancer was doing. A couple of times the mare bucked while cantering, and once she trotted right over the low dressage-ring rail. "You get right back in there, you bad, bad girl," Stevie commanded, not missing a beat. "May I remind you that dressage takes place *within the ring!*"

When Carole had stopped sputtering with laughter, she told Stevie to try the movement again, this time keeping her outside rein tighter and her outside leg firm so that Prancer couldn't bow away from her.

"Good advice, Carole," Max commented. He and Mrs. Reg had come outside and had been observing the "lesson" quietly.

Carole spun around. "Thanks, Max. We thought we'd

kill two birds with one stone, having Stevie and Prancer both get practice."

"And you are—?" Max inquired.

Carole grinned sheepishly. "I'm helping them out. I'm the 'stage coach.'"

Max and Mrs. Reg laughed. "I've often said that riding a dressage test is like being onstage," Mrs. Reg commented.

Carole grinned at the older woman gratefully. Mrs. Reg could be as tough as her son, but she was always helping out in a pinch and making them feel good about their Saddle Club plans and projects.

"It's a nice idea, and *they're* obviously learning a lot, but . . ." Max let his voice trail off.

"But?" Carole asked, fearing the worst.

Max looked at her directly. "I hate to say it, Carole, but you know as well as I do that Lisa should be the one riding that horse. She needs as much ring time as possible before the rally, and instead she's getting less than usual."

Remembering her promise to Lisa the night before, Carole tried to defend her friend. "I know, Max, and so does she. At least Prancer's getting ridden. That should help get her ready. And Lisa's really trying to get here as often as possible."

Max looked unconvinced. In a kind but firm voice he

remarked, *"Trying* to do something isn't always enough, especially when it comes to riding horses."

Reluctantly, Carole nodded. She knew anything else she said or did would sound like a lame excuse.

Max and Mrs. Reg watched Stevie and Prancer for a while longer. They seemed to enjoy seeing the feisty pair in action as much as Carole. For her part Stevie liked having an audience. She rode as well as she could for the Regnerys. Finally Max excused himself to go give a lesson. Before he left, he complimented Carole once again on her good teaching.

"I think I'll stick around to watch the end of the lesson," Mrs. Reg said, her eyes sparkling.

Carole was flattered that Mrs. Reg referred to their schooling session as a lesson. She felt even better when Mrs. Reg put an arm around her and whispered, "Maybe trying isn't everything, but it sure can help!"

"Oh, thank you, Mrs. Reg!" she cried. Across the ring Prancer used the sudden, loud noise as an excuse to shy. Stevie's good-natured rebuke brought her right back into line.

Back at the stable Stevie peeled off her riding clothes exhaustedly. "Boy, do I pity your future students," she announced to Carole. They were sitting in the locker room with Mrs. Reg, enjoying the rosy-cheeked glow that came from riding outdoors in autumn.

Carole rolled her eyes while Mrs. Reg laughed. "I remember watching Max teach his first group lesson. He was about sixteen and had just started getting paid by his father for teaching here. It was a group of little girls on ponies. Anyway, about halfway through the hour, they came into the middle of the ring and told him that they were all either going to faint, be sick, or fall off within the next five minutes, so could they please take a thirty-second break before any of those things happened."

"Was I that bad?" Carole asked when the giggling had quieted down.

"Worse," Stevie said. "Today I came several inches closer to being permanently bowlegged."

It was great to sit and chat with Mrs. Reg. The Saddle Club rarely had a chance just to hang out with her. When they did, it was special and entertaining. They never knew when she would launch into one of her Max stories or share a Pine Hollow secret. Both Carole and Stevie knew that she had something on her mind, though, or she would have been hurrying off to take care of Pine Hollow affairs that kept her endlessly occupied. Sure enough, as soon as Stevie had changed, she got down to business.

"Now, girls," she began. Stevie and Carole both looked up at the serious tone of her voice. "I know you've been busy with the riding part of this rally, but I wanted to remind you that you've got the whole rest of the day to think about. And that means—" She paused to let one of the girls supply the end of the sentence.

"Stable management," they said in unison.

"Yes. Exactly. Stable management. Which means health records, feeding schedules, loading the van, and tack and turnout, among other things."

"Has Max picked a stable manager yet?" Carole asked. Usually, all of this organizing was supervised by the nonriding member of the team. Everyone was expected to clean her own tack, bathe her own horse, and provide the personal information necessary, but the stable manager pitched in and acted like everyone's mother in the weeks before the rally. This rally had been planned so hastily that they hadn't finalized who would take on the job.

"I thought one of the younger kids was going to do it," Stevie mentioned, recalling Max's suggestion from the first dressage rally meeting.

"That's a fine idea," Mrs. Reg said. "But you guys have got to get cracking and pick someone. Forget May Grover. It's her birthday that Saturday, and she's having a big party. In fact, you may have to forget most of the little kids—I think she's invited all of Willow Creek. Personally, I'd rather go with someone more experienced, anyway. A lot of the unrateds and D-ones haven't ever been to a rally before."

"You've got a point, Mrs. Reg," Carole conceded. "Besides, sometimes May and her friends seem to have enough trouble organizing themselves for lessons, let alone organizing all of us for a regional rally. Half the time they show up for class without their hard hats or crops."

"Exactly," Mrs. Reg said. "So choose wisely, and be prepared to do a good deal of the work yourselves. In the meantime let's see checklists for everything. This is a real rally, you know, even though there's no cross-country or stadium." Mrs. Reg gave them both an encouraging grin before heading out to her office.

When she was safely out of earshot, Stevie groaned. "Was it my imagination, or did she just give us the classic Mrs. Reg I'm-relying-on-you-girls-to-take-charge-or-else look?"

"She gave us the look, all right," Carole replied dully. "Too bad she didn't tell us one of her stories. At least then we could have pretended we didn't have the slightest idea what she was talking about."

Stevie nodded. She and Carole both stared at the floor glumly. It seemed as if the rally were taking over their whole lives. Just when they thought they had made progress in one area—getting Prancer ready to compete —Mrs. Reg reminded them about another area that they had been completely neglecting. Obviously she was counting on them. Veronica was never any help in stable management. Betsy and Polly were cooperative and helpful teammates, but they were lazy about cleaning tack. They tended to skimp on things unless someone got after them.

"But we're no good at this sort of thing, either," Carole said.

"You mean I'm no good at it, right?" Stevie asked. She knew she wasn't exactly famous for her untamed enthusiasm for the nittier, grittier side of riding and the stable-management book work.

"No, I really do mean we," Carole insisted. "I love doing all that stuff on my own for Starlight, but I can never seem to get everyone else as excited as I am."

"And with people doubling up on practice already, it's going to be even harder."

"Maybe Betsy will take over," Carole suggested hopefully.

"Maybe," Stevie said.

"Her little sister might want to be stable manager," Carole pointed out.

"Her little sister is six and hates riding," Stevie said.

"Oh," Carole said.

After staring into space for a minute or two more, they got up to go. There was still an hour of daylight left for Carole to ride.

"Look on the bright side," Stevie said as they went to the tack room. "Prancer *is* doing much better."

"And you are, too," Carole added. At least one part of their Saddle Club project was working. It was just that there suddenly seemed to be about ninety-nine other parts.

"Disgusting," Stevie commented. She was examining Topside's bit before putting it in his mouth. As she suspected, it was coated with scum.

"What?" Carole asked. She had Starlight all tacked up for their special Saturday Horse Wise practice and was waiting for Stevie to join her. Both of them were crossing their fingers that Lisa would show up in the next five minutes.

"Topside's bit is greener than a pasture in June," Stevie said succinctly.

"Add it to your list," Carole said. Since their talk with Mrs. Reg, the two girls had been making mental checklists of what things needed cleaning, organizing, pitching, and/or replacing. Unfortunately, there weren't many things that *didn't* need cleaning, organizing, pitching, and/or replacing.

"My list's so long I forget what's on it," Stevie wailed.

Carole nodded sympathetically. "I know—mine too." She paused, pressing her lips into a thin, determined line. "After Horse Wise today we are going to have that stable-management meeting with everyone going to the rally, or else. We just can't keep track of everything—it's too much."

As they led Starlight and Topside out to the mounting block, Lisa came running into the stable. "Phew! Made it! I'll be out in ten minutes!" she exclaimed.

"Make that five—Prancer's tacked up and waiting in her stall!" Carole called after her.

Lisa spun around, incredulous. "You—?" She didn't have to elaborate any further.

"Yup, we did," Stevie said.

"How can I ever thank—" Lisa began.

Carole interrupted with more news. "Stevie's also been riding Prancer, and I've been coaching the two of them."

Lisa stood speechless for a moment. Then she threw down her bag and embraced both of them in a bear hug. "You're the best! You're the absolute best!"

She was totally overwhelmed that her friends had taken the time and trouble not only to groom and tack up her horse but also to school her. Lisa had been wondering all week whether Prancer would be skittish after having two days off. Instead, the mare had been having training sessions with two experienced riders. She had also been wondering about something else all week: whether she should quit the play altogether. The more she tried to fine-tune her schedule, the more desperate for time she felt. And she was *not* going to sacrifice Prancer's chances. But now, thanks to Carole and Stevie, it looked as if she wouldn't have to, even if she stayed in the play.

"We know we're the best," Stevie said. "We hear that all the time—from Max, Mrs. Reg, Olympic coaches. . . . Now get going and get out here."

"*Five* minutes!" Lisa promised.

Outdoors in the dressage ring Max had already begun watching riders go through their tests. Mrs. Reg was standing outside the ring. She had copies of all of the tests in her hands and would prompt anyone who forgot hers. Today Max wanted to see the performances in their entirety, to see if breaking them up and working on the hard parts had helped. This would also enable him to plan the remaining lessons before the rally. Several minutes earlier Carole had overheard him joke to Mrs. Reg: "If everyone's perfect, we'll just spend next week trail riding."

"You remember that, boy," she told Starlight as she walked him on a loose rein to relax them both. She had volunteered to follow Veronica on Garnet, who, she had to admit, were doing quite nicely. Lisa would go next and then Stevie. Carole stole a glance at Topside. He looked wonderful, and Stevie was riding more attentively, thanks to being woken up by Prancer. If only Lisa would do as well.

Carole warmed up efficiently and was ready when Veronica saluted Max a second time. Starlight was getting used to the size of the small ring. He remained quiet but alert as they circled twice around, preparing to enter. In the first movement of the test, however, Carole tensed up and forgot to keep her leg on. The halt was late and uneven. Sternly she reminded herself that Max had told them that every movement counted. If one was horrible, the next one could still be a seven or an eight. "I will not let one bad halt ruin the whole test," she told herself. Her determination paid off. The rest of the ride went smoothly. The only other major mistake was her forgetting the end of the test and having to be prompted by Mrs. Reg.

As she exited, Max barked out his comments: "Mostly accurate. Good transitions. Watch the first halt. Next please." He didn't bother to correct her for the obvious mistake of memory failure. Carole sighed in relief. She had talked herself out of a tough spot, and it had worked.

Lisa gave Carole the thumbs-up sign on Carole's way

out. Lisa had only had a few minutes to warm up, and she felt rushed and under pressure. As quickly as possible after her ride, she'd have to get back to WCCT.

After another turn around the ring, Lisa urged Prancer forward, and they entered at a smart trot. Then they halted promptly and squarely. Carole stole a glance back in Max's direction and saw the trace of a smile on his lips. By her entrance alone it was easy to see what a wonderful dressage horse Prancer might be someday. She had an eye-catching trot and carried herself beautifully.

Unfortunately, her entrance alone had to serve as proof of her potential. Unlike Carole's first halt, Lisa's turned out to be the best moment in her test. As soon as she turned the corner at C, Lisa seemed to lose all confidence. The others watched as she sat frozen in the saddle, a stricken look on her face. Prancer was behaving fine, but Lisa seemed nervous all the same. She gave every aid about three strides too late. When she did ask for a new gait, she overdid it, sending Prancer leaping forward into a canter instead of quietly picking up a trot. Midway through the ride Lisa halted at the side of the ring. "May I start over, Max?" she asked, her voice quavering.

Max agreed readily.

Lisa walked quietly for a few minutes, organizing her thoughts. She felt stiff all over. Her neck ached from stress, and her legs felt cramped from the long choreography rehearsal they'd had at WCCT the day before. "I won't let you down," she whispered fiercely to Prancer, stroking her neck. Silently she reminded herself that she couldn't disappoint Stevie and Carole, who had worked so hard to help her, or Max, who had been so patient. She took a deep breath and started over.

She hadn't thought things could go any worse, but she was wrong. Before, Prancer had sensed Lisa's nervousness. Now she decided to take advantage of it. She trotted right through the halting point, ignoring Lisa's snatches at the reins. When she did halt, she fussed with the bit. At the far corner she shied at her own shadow and refused to settle down. This time Max was the first to speak. "Why don't you warm up a bit more, Lisa?" he suggested. "You can ride your test last."

Suddenly more determined than nervous, Lisa brought the mare to a halt by sheer willpower. Mrs. Spitz would have a fit if Lisa showed up to rehearsal that late. "I can't ride last, Max. I just can't today. I'm sure it will go better now. Can't I try?" she pleaded.

Max came over to Prancer's side. In a quiet voice, so that no one could overhear, he asked, "What do you think is going wrong today, Lisa?"

Lisa stuck out her lower lip stubbornly. "I don't know."

"Perhaps if you spent more time riding, the test would go better," he said gently.

88

"I'm doing everything I can!" Lisa wailed. "I have a schedule to keep, but it's getting harder and harder to stick to it. The only reason I could come to Pony Club today is that the director is working with the chorus for an hour and then with the adult leads for a half hour. She gave me permission to come to Horse Wise until noon, and it's not much time, but it's all I've got! It's absolutely all I've got!"

There was a pause as Lisa's words hung in the air. Then Veronica diAngelo's sharp voice demanded, "I guess we should all feel blessed by your presence, huh? *Grateful* that you could make it at all, right?"

Lisa bit her lip for an instant, her face distraught. All at once she burst into hysterical tears. Turning Prancer toward the barn, she urged her into a trot and fled the scene.

"Polly, why don't you ride next?" Max suggested quietly. He nodded to Carole and Stevie that they could go after Lisa.

Lisa pulled up beside the stable doors and jumped off. She buried her face in Prancer's neck, sobbing. Seeing her standing there, Red O'Malley put down the bale of hay he was carrying and went to find out what was wrong.

"I'll put Prancer away for you. You just try to calm yourself," he told Lisa, taking the mare's reins.

Lisa was too upset to protest. All day—all week—she

had been on the brink of bursting into tears. Veronica's comment had been the last straw. She had been trying her hardest to please everyone, and instead it seemed as if all she got was criticism from every side. What could she do now? She was so confused, she couldn't think straight anymore. She had to get away—from Pine Hollow, WCCT, everything. Choking back tears, Lisa ran blindly toward the woods behind the barn as fast as she could.

"ANY SIGN OF her?" Carole called hopefully. She was holding Starlight and Topside while Stevie took a look around for Lisa.

"Not a trace," Stevie answered, emerging from the tack room. "And Red said he had volunteered to put Prancer away for her."

"Then I guess we'd better get back to the lesson," Carole said after a pause.

Stevie nodded glumly. Neither she nor Carole seemed to want to guess where Lisa had vanished to in such a hurry. Admitting that she had left Pine Hollow to go to rehearsal would be the same as admitting that she was going to choose acting. For good. And neither of them was ready to admit that.

"ONE MORE CANTER, one more trot, and then we're
through, boy," Stevie murmured.

After Lisa's departure she had remounted Topside and
begun her dressage test. Topside was behaving beautifully, as usual. Stevie didn't like to be cocky—or at least
not too cocky—but she couldn't help thinking that they
were having the best ride of anyone in the class. The
gelding's black tail swung rhythmically in the sun as
they trotted down the long side. He looked confident,
and so did Stevie.

"One-two, one-two," she hummed to herself. "Steady
as a rock, that's right, boy, one-two, one-two." On the
exact moment that they crossed the letter A, Topside
cantered. His canter was so smooth that all Stevie had

to do was sit up straight and think about her own position. She imagined that she was a grand prix rider at the Olympics. When they came down the center line, Stevie was actually a little sorry that her ride was over. She had to turn back into a D-3 Pony Clubber as soon as she saluted.

"As good as I would expect on a horse like Topside," Max commented.

Stevie took his judgment as a compliment.

"Ride like that in a week, and you're sure to get a low score," Betsy said.

"That was great, Stevie," Polly added.

Stevie thanked them both. She was about ready to launch into a long discourse on the merits of riding a great horse like Topside when Carole cut her short. "Speaking of getting a low score, everyone meet in the locker room after getting untacked to talk stable management. If we don't get organized soon, we could be the best riders in the region and still finish last."

"That may be the case, but I won't be able to make it, unfortunately," Veronica announced. "You can be assured that my tack and turnout and personal grooming will be as immaculate as always. Mother's sending a man over to do Garnet on Friday, and I've just bought a new stock tie, ratcatcher, and coat."

"Boy, that's really the Pony Club spirit," Carole grumbled.

"No new breeches?" Stevie asked sarcastically.

Veronica gave her a withering glance. "I've only worn my old ones once—I think they'll do."

"Where are you off to in such a hurry?" Carole asked.

"Oh, nowhere in particular," Veronica replied airily. "But if certain people don't have to stay for the riding part, why should I have to stay for the stable-management meeting?" With that she wheeled Garnet and headed for the barn.

"Unbelievable," Carole muttered, staring after her angrily.

"No—just Veronicable," Stevie replied.

CAROLE PUT STARLIGHT away quickly. There was no time today to linger over combing out his tail and painting on hoof polish: She had a rally team to organize. She decided to get a jump start on the meeting by walking around and catching people while they were untacking to ask them for their completed feeding schedules and equipment checklists.

It didn't take long. First Betsy, then Polly, and finally, Stevie, told her that they hadn't *quite* finished doing the charts. Resignedly Carole told them just to hurry and meet in the locker room as soon as possible. While she waited for the three girls, she took a pencil stub from her pocket and scribbled an equipment list. It didn't look too bad. Everything was pretty straightforward and could probably be scrounged from Pine Hollow.

As soon as they had all gathered, Carole began to read from the list. She told them to copy everything down. "Okay. First, the obvious: bridle, saddle, saddle pad, hat, boots, coat, shirt—"

"Excuse me, but why isn't the stable manager taking care of all this?" Polly asked.

"The stable manager isn't taking care of all this because there is no stable manager yet. If you'll remember, we're supposed to be getting a younger member of Horse Wise to help out," Carole replied a little impatiently. "Unfortunately, May Grover's birthday falls on the same weekend as dressage rally, and every young equestrienne in the state of Virginia is invited to a slumber party Friday night. So we're still looking. Any suggestions?"

"Um, well—no," Polly replied.

"Fine. Then let's go on. Where was I? Oh, yeah. Saddle, saddle pad, hat, boots—"

"Excuse me, but are we going to have gray-and-green Horse Wise saddle pads under our regular ones like last time?" Betsy asked.

Carole frowned. She wasn't sure. Usually they wore matching pads in Horse Wise's colors at competitions, but no one had mentioned it. "I'll have to ask Mrs. Reg," she said, writing a note to herself.

"Don't forget to ask her about the Horse Wise banner, while you're at it," Betsy reminded her.

"Right," Carole said. "Okay, coat, shirt—"

"Do we wear our black coats and stock ties since it's a dressage rally?" Polly asked.

Carole bit her lip. She wasn't positive about that one, either. Dressing herself for a show had never been Carole's strong point.

"If we do, I'm in trouble because I don't have a black coat," Betsy said.

Carole smiled. She had an answer. "You can use the Pine Hollow spare," she said. Over the years Mrs. Reg had kept a collection of all the garments riders had abandoned or forgotten so that they could be used in a pinch.

"But *I* was counting on using the spare—I used it for combined training rally last year," Polly wailed.

Carole glared at her. "All right. I will ask Mrs. Reg," she said through gritted teeth. "Now, may I continue? We will also need grooming kits assembled according to United States Pony Club standards—and that means all the brushes have to be spotless—as well as the team first-aid kit that we always take. Also—"

"Uh, Carole?" Stevie asked timidly.

"Yes?"

"I hate to say it, but someone's going to have to buy and stock a whole new first-aid kit."

"And why is that, Stevie?" Carole inquired.

"Because the old one got lost on the overnight trail ride."

"I see," Carole said calmly. She smiled calmly. She calmly held up the piece of paper with the list on it. Then she calmly tore it into a hundred tiny pieces and calmly threw them up into the air.

"Uh, Carole?" Stevie asked.

"Yes, Stevie."

"Should we take this as a sign that you're through with organizing the stable management?"

"In a word, Stevie, yes, *I QUIT!*" Carole cried.

Stevie knew a crisis when she saw one. She was so used to getting herself into them that she could often help other people get out of them. The Horse Wise Pony Club was facing a dressage-rally crisis that had to be solved immediately.

"All right," Stevie said, jumping to her feet. "Here's my solution. Everyone takes care of her own stuff—equipment, horse, clothes—everything. The stable manager—when we find one—will be there on the day of the show to help out, but we have to get ourselves ready. And we can't bother Mrs. Reg, either. She's already volunteered to drive the van. Okay? Does everyone agree?"

"That still doesn't solve the problem of who's going to organize the team equipment," Betsy pointed out.

"How about you?" Stevie asked. She had decided that it was too late in the game to beat around the bush.

"Me? If anyone should, it should be you. *You've* got the wonder horse. *You* don't even have to practice," Betsy said.

Stevie opened her mouth to object, but Polly cut her off. "What about Veronica? She doesn't have to practice, groom her own horse, or anything. Make her do it."

"If she does it, it obviously won't get done," Carole said.

"You know, this rally is turning into one huge hassle," Betsy commented.

"Nobody said you had to go!" Stevie retorted.

"Fine! Maybe I won't—if it would make you so happy!" Betsy cried.

The door to the locker room swung open. All four girls froze. Mrs. Reg's kindly face peeked in. "Oh, good. I was sure you were here somewhere, preparing for next weekend. Keep up the good work, girls. Max and I expect great things from you. I'll be off now. I don't want to interrupt anymore."

Carole, Stevie, Betsy, and Polly looked at one another self-consciously after the door closed again.

"Why don't we talk about it tomorrow?" Polly suggested.

"Sounds good," Stevie said.

"Yeah, see you guys tomorrow," Carole added. She

started to gather up her stuff quickly. Suddenly they were all in a hurry to leave.

"TD's?" Stevie whispered.

"Meet you outside in two minutes," Carole whispered back.

Sitting in the traditional Saddle Club booth at TD's still seemed wrong. After a moment's hesitation Carole and Stevie once again chose a table for two.

"Still got only two thirds of the gang, huh?" the waitress asked. This time she sounded downright sympathetic.

They nodded glumly. "You going to waste my good ice cream again?" she asked Stevie.

"I think I can manage a dish of blueberry with marshmallow topping," Stevie muttered.

"Make mine a chocolate cone, please," Carole said despondently.

The waitress looked at the two of them and shook her head. "Hope the lost sheep comes back to the flock soon, girls," she said.

"Thanks," they said together.

This time they did manage to finish their ice cream—even faster than usual, since they hardly spent any time talking. "Maybe if we—" Carole began.

"Yeah?" Stevie asked.

"Nothing," Carole said. They stared into space for a few minutes.

"How about—" Stevie paused. Carole raised her eyebrows. "Nah," Stevie said.

Finally Carole suggested, "Let's give Lisa a ring and see how she's doing. I'll bet she's calmed down by now. Maybe she has time to meet us—just for five minutes."

Stevie was doubtful, but they decided to try. They got change for the pay phone from the waitress and dialed Lisa's home number. Mrs. Atwood answered. "Is Lisa there?" Stevie inquired.

"You mean she's not with you?" Lisa's mother asked.

"Us? No, she left Pine Hollow hours ago," Stevie said.

"But I thought for sure she'd be with you because the director of the play has called three times looking for her," Mrs. Atwood explained.

"You mean she's not at rehearsal?" Carole demanded.

"No, she never showed up." Mrs. Atwood was beginning to sound concerned. "Do you have any idea where she might have gone after she left Pine Hollow?"

Stevie told Carole that Lisa was missing, but they both knew the answer. If Lisa wasn't at home or at the theater or at Pine Hollow, there was only one other place she could be.

"Don't worry, Mrs. Atwood. We know where to find her," Stevie said.

ONCE THEY FIGURED out where Lisa was, Carole and Stevie were all business. They practically flew back to Pine Hollow, grabbed their hats, and put bridles on Starlight and Topside. It was an unwritten Saddle Club rule that for a quick trip through the woods, bareback was the way to go. "Race you to the creek!" Stevie called, and they were off.

Both horses were thrilled to be out of the dressage ring, cantering side by side through the back pasture and onto the trail. Stevie and Carole urged them on. They reached the creek in no time at all.

"Shh!" Carole put a finger to her lips and pointed. Lisa was sitting on the big rock, her legs tucked up under her and her face in her hands. They could hear her muttering to herself in between sobs. "Can't ride, can't act, failing all my classes," she was saying.

At that last comment Stevie and Carole couldn't help smiling. Lisa was incapable of getting a B. Even if she had handed in a blank page with her name at the top, her teachers probably would have given her an A out of habit.

Unaware of their presence, Lisa stared down at the running water. In her heart of hearts she had known, practically since the day she had first mapped out her schedule, that there was no way she was going to be able to ride in the rally and be Annie. She hadn't wanted to admit it to herself then, but now she had to. Stevie and Carole would want her to quit the play so she could ride with them as usual, and why shouldn't she? Hollie would be a great Annie. She even deserved the part more than Lisa. And Lisa could forget all about WCCT, mean Anna Henchman, long rehearsals. And, she thought sadly, she could forget being up under the lights, wearing her Annie costume, and having her parents and friends in the audience clapping wildly for her. Yes, she could forget acting altogether.

Stevie and Carole might have stood there watching her till night fell if Topside hadn't taken the opportunity to nip Starlight, who squealed indignantly.

Lisa looked up. Her face was red, blotchy, and tear-stained. Stevie and Carole dismounted and walked toward her.

"Phew! I'm glad you're here," Stevie said brightly. "We thought a Broadway director might have whisked you off to New York for a starring role."

"Fat chance. At the rate I'm going, the only starring role I'm up for is that of Queen Failure," Lisa said bitterly. "Failure at Pony Club. Failure at *Annie*. Failure at school . . ."

Stevie jumped to attention. She was not going to let Lisa get away with putting herself down anymore. "First of all, by 'failure at school,' you probably mean you got, what, a couple of A-minuses?"

"Well, actually only one," Lisa conceded sheepishly.

"Well, let me tell you—I would love to bring home that kind of failure to my mom and dad, because they would post that kind of failure on the refrigerator door," Stevie said. "And secondly, if I had started riding when you did, I'd be lucky if I knew what Pony Club meant! And as for my famous career as star of stage and screen, let's just say our home movies are embarrassing enough!"

The beginnings of a smile played on Lisa's lips, but she kept her eyes downcast. Stevie thought fast. "Hey, look at me! Remember that time I tried to do a hundred things at once?"

Lisa nodded. No one in The Saddle Club would ever forget Stevie's attempt to organize the school fair, run the hospital fund-raiser, and head up the student-government election, at the same time that a group of Italian boys were visiting. Watching her juggle all her commitments had been better than a three-ring circus.

"But *you* managed to do everything successfully, whereas I can't even do two things," Lisa pointed out. "The past two weeks—"

"The past two weeks you've been way overcommitted," Carole finished for her. "When Stevie did all those things, she didn't have to worry about learning a whole new skill."

"That's right—I had all the skills I needed: getting into trouble and having fun," Stevie joked.

At Lisa's wan smile, Carole hurried on with her pep talk. "No one ever said acting was easy, you know. But you walked in out of the blue and got the lead."

"Sometimes I wish I'd never auditioned," Lisa said, her voice threatening to crack again. "This is such a familiar feeling—being a beginner. Everyone else seems to have been born riding or acting."

Carole and Stevie nodded sympathetically. Lisa was such a good rider now that both of them had practically forgotten that she had come to Pine Hollow less experienced than they were.

"At least I'm over the hump in riding," Lisa said. "I don't have to ask what a martingale is or how to pick out a hoof anymore. I can't even remember not knowing.

103

But being in *Annie* is like that time my French class went to Montreal. Everyone looks at you funny because you can hardly speak the language. At first it's fun. But pretty soon you want to go home to Willow Creek—or Pine Hollow."

"You mean you're not going to quit riding, after all?" Carole asked.

"Quit riding?" Lisa repeated incredulously. "What ever gave you that idea?"

"We, ah—" Carole began sheepishly. She wasn't quite sure how to explain their worry to Lisa.

"We thought you might have so much fun acting that you'd decide you liked the stage better than horses and that you'd want to be in a lot more plays. And then you'd start hanging around with the theater crowd at school, and pretty soon you'd get a personal acting coach and join a mime troupe and run off to Hollywood to star in movies and forget our names when we asked you for autographs," Stevie explained.

"Or at least want to be in a lot more plays," Carole said.

For the second time that day Lisa was overwhelmed by her friends' concern. She could hardly believe they'd been so worried she would quit riding. Her only thought lately had been how much she missed Pine Hollow and The Saddle Club and how she could get through the play without disappointing her friends, Max, and the rally team anymore. Well, her decision to quit the play would prove, once and for all—to them and herself—that she was truly devoted to riding. "That does it," Lisa said. "I'm going to give up the part."

"What?" Stevie and Carole cried in unison.

"I'm dropping out of WCCT," Lisa said.

"But what about all the people counting on you to play Annie?" Carole asked.

"They'll find someone else. I don't want to let you and Max and Mrs. Reg and Prancer down," Lisa said. "Besides, my true loyalty is to The Saddle Club and riding, and dropping out will prove it."

"True loyalty? But this isn't a *life* choice," Stevie reminded her. "It's just to help you get through the next two weeks."

Lisa stared hard at Stevie. Could it be as simple as that? Had she really blown the whole dilemma way out of proportion? What Stevie said was true: In reality the decision *would* only affect fourteen days of her life.

"Yeah, and what about all those lines you memorized?" Carole was saying.

"But I'd be able to memorize my dressage tests instead," Lisa heard herself answering, but already her protests seemed feeble.

"But—but—this is your big chance!" Stevie cried.

"It's Prancer's big chance, too—to prove she can do dressage," Lisa said.

"She'll have other chances," Carole said flatly.

"And how do you know you'll get another lead? Actors can wait years for this kind of thing," Stevie said indignantly.

Lisa laughed out loud. Carole and Stevie were actually upset with her saying she would bow out of the play. "Is this The Saddle Club talking?" she asked. "Because it sounds like the Willow Creek Community Theater."

Carole and Stevie did not seem to find anything funny. "You've got a part to play, missy, and don't you forget it," Stevie said.

"What happened to 'The show must go on' and all that?" Carole asked.

"All right! All right! You win! I'll play Annie!" Lisa practically shouted. Carole and Stevie shouted and hugged her in excitement and began talking excitely about coming to see her in the play.

Lisa breathed a huge inner sigh of relief. Suddenly everything had fallen into place, thanks to talking with her friends. She *had* put a lot of work into *Annie* already. And there was no point in breaking her commitment to WCCT. She would do the play, after all—which would probably be a lot of fun—and then get back to riding right afterward. She and Prancer would have a chance before too long. It *would* be hard not to take part in the rally. She would probably feel left out. "I guess I can still help out behind the scenes, though," Lisa mused aloud.

Carole and Stevie nodded. Then they seemed to do a double take. Carole's jaw dropped. Stevie's eyes opened wide. A perfect solution to the dressage team's disorganization and Lisa's wanting to participate was staring them in the face. "Behind the scenes? Behind the scenes? How could we be such idiots?" Stevie cried.

"You're telling me!" Carole exclaimed.

Lisa was now utterly confused. "Would someone mind telling me why my helping out behind the scenes makes you two idiots?" she asked.

"Never mind. You've got a rehearsal to get to. We'll talk tonight," Stevie decided.

"Right. Your house, okay, Lisa? At nine-twelve, that is? We'll come over," Carole said.

Lisa grinned. She *was* still on top of things, after all. "Actually, today is Saturday, so my free time is later. It's nine forty-four tonight," she said, trying to sound casual.

"Boy, you've really let your schedule go to pot. You can hardly remember a thing," Stevie kidded her.

"Anyway, would someone mind informing me what we're going to be discussing? I am giving up twelve precious minutes, after all," Lisa joked.

Stevie and Carole were both about to burst with their idea. They knew Lisa should be on her way, though, and they didn't want to delay her anymore. Besides, they knew that as soon as they told her the plan, the three of them would simply have to discuss it in detail.

"Listen," Carole said, "I'm going to leave it at this: There just might be a way you can still be involved in the rally. In fact, I'm ninety-nine percent sure."

"How?" Lisa cried.

"You'll find out at nine forty-four," she answered. With a grin she added, "And I guarantee one thing: Things will look better tomorrow."

"But that's what I'm supposed to say!" Lisa cried. The three of them laughed. It did sound funny to hear Carole giving Lisa's advice—or Annie's—to Annie!

Lisa tried to talk them into telling her the news right away, but Carole and Stevie remained as adamant as two hardened stage mothers. "But it's pointless for me to go to rehearsal now. I'm already very late, and it's almost an hour's walk to the high school from here," Lisa said.

Carole looked from her to Stevie. "Stevie, do you notice any faster means of transportation around here?" she asked.

"Oh, you mean like a bus or a train or something like that?" Stevie asked, playing dumb.

"Yeah, like a bus or a train, but, well, different."

"I don't know about you, but I've always found a horse could travel cross-country pretty fast."

"Funny, I've found that, too."

"You know what else is great about riding?" Stevie asked.

"No, what?"

"It really annoys foolish people who don't like the smell of horses."

"I must say that *is* an added bonus."

Lisa stood up and put her hands on her hips, fixing them with a mock glare. "All right," she asked, "who's going to give me a leg up?"

In a flash Carole tossed Lisa up on Starlight and Stevie up on Topside. Then she found a tree stump and hopped on herself, in front of Lisa. "Anna Henchman, here we come!" Stevie yelled.

It took them ten minutes to ride from the creek to the high-school playing fields. On the way the horses had to splash through a few streams, and the girls got partially soaked. When they hit the fields, Carole and Stevie let them out all the way. They tore across the fields.

"Are those people in the play?" Carole called back, pointing.

Lisa stared ahead at the school building. Sure enough, the entire cast was standing outside the auditorium, taking their midrehearsal break. For a split second Lisa felt embarrassed. Then she thought of the entrance she was making as she and her two best friends, mounted on two practically matched bay Thoroughbreds, streaked toward the doors, manes and tails flying. Sensing the importance of the moment, Carole added the extra touch of pulling Starlight up just in the nick of time, like a cowboy in an old Western.

"Sorry I'm late," Lisa announced to the group, hopping off smartly, "but I like to make a dramatic entrance."

The cast burst into spontaneous applause, whooping and cheering. Carole and Stevie nodded to one another and, as if on cue, took off back across the fields.

Mr. Ryan put a hand up to his eyes to shield them from the sun. "Who were those masked girls?" he asked.

"Why, that was the Lone Ranger," Hollie joked.

"All right, enough already," Mrs. Spitz said when the laughter had died down. She sent everyone back into the auditorium except Lisa.

"Mrs. Spitz? I really am sorry I'm late," Lisa said.

Mrs. Spitz looked down at Lisa seriously. "Is this going to be the last time?" she asked. Lisa nodded as vigorously as she could. "Then, look. I've said it before, and I'll say it again. I know you've been under a lot of pressure, but I still think you're going to do a wonderful job as Annie."

"I know I will," Lisa promised. "But it's not just because of me. It's because I've got the best coaches in the world."

"Drama coaches?" Mrs. Spitz asked.

"Not *exactly*," Lisa said.

At exactly nine forty-three Carole and Stevie rang the Atwood doorbell. They had commandeered Colonel Hanson into giving them a ride over. He had also supplied a tray of marshmallow crispies for the meeting. All three of them had waited in the car for five minutes, not wanting to disturb Lisa. They had decided to ring one minute early, so that they could catch her right as she started her break.

Mrs. Atwood opened the door right away. "Good timing, girls. You've got thirty seconds to get up to her bedroom. Now, scoot!" Lisa and Carole didn't have to be told twice. Before Mrs. Atwood could finish asking Colonel Hanson to come in for coffee, they were through the door. They knew the layout of the Atwood house by heart and were up the stairs in an instant. Like a herd of wild horses, they thundered down the hallway to Lisa's room.

"Open up! Committee to Save Lisa Atwood's Life as a Pony Clubber!" Stevie announced, banging on the door.

Inside the room they heard Lisa counting, "Five, four, three, two, one—open sesame!"

Carole and Stevie burst inside, both talking a mile a minute. Lisa tried to interrupt to tell them she couldn't listen to both of them at once, but they refused to allow her to talk. "We only have twelve minutes! No, eleven!" Stevie said.

By the time they were down to eight, two things had become clear to Lisa. First, the team was currently a disorganized mess because nobody had had time to get her own things together, let alone work on gathering the communal equipment. And second, the dressage team desperately needed help.

"So if I have this right, what you're saying is—" Lisa started to say.

"What we're saying is, can that computer of yours print out equipment checklists and feeding schedules as well as history papers because *we want you to be the stable manager!*" Stevie finished.

Lisa looked at her two friends. Her day had had as many highs and lows as the roller coaster at the amusement park. And it was ending on the highest peak yet.

112

"So?" Carole asked.

"So? So! So I say since you guys got the news out in four minutes, we still have eight to celebrate in! Break out the marshmallow crispies!" Lisa cried.

"Yippee-hi-yi-yay!" Stevie whooped.

The Saddle Club made good use of the time allowed. They did an impromptu dance around Lisa's room—which involved screaming for joy and tossing stuffed animals in the air—flopped down onto her bed, and ate about six crispies apiece.

"This really is the perfect solution," Lisa said, chewing on a treat. "I have *some* time to devote to the rally—I just can't be responsible for getting Prancer ready. As stable manager I'll only have to answer to you guys."

"More like we'll have to answer to you," Stevie pointed out.

"And even though you're not riding, you're still making a huge contribution to the team," Carole said.

"Boy, will Max and Mrs. Reg be thrilled. Especially Mrs. Reg. The poor woman walked in on us and Polly and Betsy when we were on the brink of a knockdown, drag-out fight over who was going to buy the new first-aid kit!" Stevie exclaimed.

"Consider it bought," Lisa said. She dashed off a note to herself on a memo pad. Carole and Stevie leaned back on their pillows and grinned from ear to ear. They felt relieved already, knowing that Lisa, the most organized and efficient member of The Saddle Club—and probably of Horse Wise, too—had taken over.

"I can just picture the beautiful checklists and schedules you'll draw up on your computer," Stevie said dreamily.

"And the clipboard you'll carry around at the rally," Carole added, sighing.

Lisa leaned over and reached under her bed. "You mean this one?" she asked. She held up a weathered clipboard with a pen attached.

"Carole," Stevie said, "our every problem is solved."

When the eight minutes were long since past, Colonel Hanson hollered up the stairs for Stevie and Carole. Lisa had decided that since she no longer had to ride, she could extend her free time by ten or fifteen minutes —or maybe even half an hour. She promised to have the forms printed out by Monday to give to Carole at school.

"BETTER AND BETTER," Carole commented appreciatively. She had just watched Stevie run through all of the transitions in her test. As usual she and Topside were in top form. The girls were having their regular Tuesday lesson. Max was down at the other end of the ring working intensively with Polly and Romeo, whose circles looked more like squares.

"Thanks," Stevie said, "but I'm not sure if we *are* better and better. Most of the time I feel like we're always the same."

Carole amended her compliment. "Okay, you're always the same, and that's always good. The judges will love him."

"Exactly," Stevie said glumly. "They'll love *him*, and *he* deserves all the praise he gets."

"I didn't mean it like that—you look great, too," Carole added hastily.

Stevie apologized. She explained that she didn't want Carole to think she was fishing for compliments, but she really and truly believed that whatever score they received, Topside would be the reason. "We might get a blue ribbon; we might not. It hardly matters. If we do, it won't be a big deal anyway. Topside will have earned it, and he's gotten blue ribbons at international competitions like the American Horse Show—what would it mean to get one at a little Pony Club rally?"

"It would mean—" Carole paused. What would it mean? She didn't know, because she'd never had Stevie's problem. She had never *expected* to get a blue. And whenever she and Starlight did well, she knew they had both worked hard.

"It's hard to answer, isn't it? The whole point of Pony Club is to learn. But I'm not learning anything. On Topside I'm just sitting back and enjoying the ride," Stevie said.

"Are you saying that you want more of a challenge?" Carole asked.

Stevie nodded, a slow grin creeping across her face. "Want—and have: I've decided to ride Prancer at the rally if it's all right with Max."

Carole clapped her hands together in excitement. "That's a great idea! It'll be wonderful for you *and* Prancer. Why didn't you just say so?"

Stevie tossed her head airily. "Oh, I wanted to build up the dramatic suspense," she said.

"Humph," Carole muttered. "Maybe you're the one who ought to be onstage."

AFTER CLASS CAROLE and Stevie walked around handing out the forms Lisa had drawn up. They felt very important—first, to have solved the club's stable-management problem, and second, to be presenting such perfect documents. Betsy and Polly oohed and aahed openly at Lisa's neat work, just as they had admired the new first-aid kit she had dropped off on her way to school.

"Wow, she thought of *everything*," Polly exclaimed.

"I know," Betsy agreed. "Who else would have remembered hair nets? My mother and I are always having a mad search at the last minute."

When Veronica got her forms, she just shrugged. "It's about time Lisa got her act together. Obviously, she wasn't going to be able to ride that wild horse off the track," she muttered.

"Oh, you mean Prancer?" Stevie asked innocently.

Veronica nodded. "Of course. That horse won't be ready to go to a show for months, let alone a Pony Club rally."

Stevie and Carole said nothing. On their way back past Garnet's stall, they noticed Veronica poring over the handouts, an impressed look on her face.

"I hope she looks like that when she hears the news about Prancer," Carole whispered.

Max and Mrs. Reg had been as thrilled as The Saddle Club predicted about the new arrangement. An expression of pure relief had passed between them. "I hated to tell you girls, but I was getting nervous about filling that spot," Mrs. Reg admitted. "Now I've no doubt you'll have the best inspections at the rally. You couldn't ask for a better stable manager. Not in the whole region."

As for Stevie's riding Prancer, Max couldn't have been more pleased. He had actually given Stevie a hug! She was so shocked that she had stood there speechless while Max exclaimed, "Good for you! Good for you, Stevie Lake!" about ten times in a row. Finally he had stepped back, looked her in the eye, and said, "We might make a horsewoman out of you yet." Stevie figured praise like that ought to keep her walking on air till the year 2025.

"Maybe more like the year 2050," Carole commented when Stevie related the news.

On their way out the two girls stopped by Mrs. Reg's office to pick up the completed forms that they had instructed everyone to drop off there. Tacked to her bulletin board was a note in Max's handwriting. *Final Dressage-Rally Teams*, it said at the top. *Horse Wise team: Carole Hanson (Starlight), Betsy Cavanaugh (Barq), Polly Giacomin (Romeo), Stephanie Lake (Prancer), Lisa Atwood (stable manager). Riding on Mixed Team with Sunny Valley PC: Veronica diAngelo (Garnet).*

"But how do you think Max decided?" Carole asked. It went without saying that they could hardly believe their luck: With Lisa stable-managing, there was only one extra Horse Wise rider, and Max had chosen to put Veronica on the mixed team.

"I think Mrs. Reg had a hand in it," Stevie answered knowingly. "Remember when she caught us fighting about the stable management? That was pretty bad, but there was one person who didn't even show up to fight! And not coming is a whole lot worse, wouldn't you say?"

"I most certainly would," a voice behind them said.

Carole and Stevie whirled around to see Mrs. Reg standing at the door. "So Veronica is not going to be on the Horse Wise team. End of story."

"But won't she—" Carole began. She had been about

to say, "Won't she throw a fit?" but had stopped herself in the interest of club spirit.

Mrs. Reg answered her unspoken question anyway. "I doubt she'll be upset. The Sunny Valley team is the home team—the host club—and they've won dressage rally two years in a row, you know. Veronica's just lucky that one of their four top riders came down with the chicken pox yesterday, and their district commissioner called me this afternoon. The truth is she has a much better chance of winning on that team," Mrs. Reg explained.

Stevie put her hands on her hips and eyed Mrs. Reg narrowly. "Them's fighting words, ma'am," she said in a Southern drawl.

"Good! A little healthy competition never hurt anyone," Mrs. Reg replied. She leaned down and put an arm around each of them. Barely whispering, she asked, "Do you want to guess who I'm rooting for?"

Carole and Stevie grinned. They didn't have to guess; they knew.

"EVERYBODY IN?" Mrs. Reg asked. She was seated in the driver's seat of the big Pine Hollow horse van. She looked at her watch anxiously. To everyone's disappointment it was overcast and raining. The foul weather had required dozens of last-minute preparations, and they were running a little late.

"Almost!" Lisa called. She had shown up at Pine Hollow at five A.M. and had been scurrying around ever since. She had grabbed rain sheets, raincoats, boot rubbers, and every spare towel or cloth she could find to fight the mud with. While Veronica loaded Garnet into the diAngelos' deluxe rig, Lisa had helped Max and Mrs. Reg load the four horses into the Pine Hollow van—including van-shy Barq, who had balked several times.

Then she had personally checked over all of the equipment one last time. Now she jumped up into the passenger-side seat of the van, clipboard in hand. "All's aboard that's going aboard, Mrs. Reg."

Mrs. Reg looked at Lisa appreciatively. "I don't know what we'd do without you, Lisa," she said. "I honestly don't." She started the engine, and the big van lumbered out of the driveway.

Thirty minutes later they pulled into the fairgrounds that Sunny Valley PC called home. The fields were a whirlwind of activity. Pony Clubbers darted from the stable area to the trailers. Parents hovered underneath the refreshment tent, drinking coffee and praying for sun. Carole, Stevie, Polly, and Betsy had ridden over to the rally with Max in Colonel Hanson's station wagon. They had staked out the Horse Wise stalls and were busy hoisting up the banner. As soon as the Pine Hollow van pulled in, they all dashed out to get their horses. Mrs. Reg helped them unload while Max gave last-minute advice. Colonel Hanson picked up the team packet with numbers, riding times, and maps. Then the three adults had to leave. The rally was beginning, and they could no longer help out, other than in an emergency. Max gathered everyone together for a final pep talk. "You've worked hard, and you deserve to be here. Ignore the rain as much as you can. Listen to what Lisa says. She's in charge. Help out anyone who needs it—on this team or any other. Think about your tests before, during, and after you ride them. Have fun out there. And good luck!"

Lisa leaned against one of the stalls as she watched Max hurry away. Later she realized that it was the only time she stopped moving all day.

THE FIRST CHALLENGE of the rally was taking the written test. Carole felt sure she had done well. "We're off to a flying start," she told the others as they handed in their tests.

"Speak for yourself," Stevie said. "I guessed on about half the questions. The last-minute studying in the car this morning paid off, though. That's how I got 'roughage,' 'bone spavin,' and the short essay on worming."

Betsy and Polly agreed. The quizzing from Max on the way over had been all the studying they had had time for. Luckily, it seemed to have done the trick. "How about the look on Veronica's face when they announced they were handing out the tests?" Polly joked. Usually she and Betsy were friendly with Veronica, but even they had gotten upset when she had skipped the stable-management meeting.

"Poor Sunny Valley," Stevie said ruefully, "how could they have known what they were getting themselves into?" She stole a glance back at Veronica, who was still working on her test—or at least still staring at the questions and her blank paper. As Stevie turned to join the rest of Horse Wise, she bumped smack into another competitor. "Excuse me, I was just—"

"Oh, *no*, excuse *me*, Miss Lake!"

Stevie whirled around. Standing in front of her was Phil Marsten. Behind him she glimpsed Cam Nelson chatting with Carole. "I didn't know *you* were representing Cross County!" Stevie said accusingly.

"Yeah, well, you didn't exactly tell me that you were on the Horse Wise team, either," Phil pointed out.

"*We* didn't even know that we were the Horse Wise team until two weeks ago," Stevie protested. "And what are *you* doing here?" she asked Cam. He had draped an arm casually over Carole's shoulders, and she was practically glowing.

Cam and Carole laughed at Stevie's accusatory tone.

"I'm competing as an individual," Cam explained. "Or I should say, Duffy and I are competing as two individuals. My home club didn't have anyone else who wanted to go."

"Naturally we met up when I decided to copy every answer off of Cam's written test," Phil joked.

Carole smiled. She was pleased that Phil had obviously remembered how well Cam had done at the Pine Hollow Know-Down.

"So why didn't Max tell you about this earlier?" Cam

asked. Carole and Stevie started to explain at the same time.

Lisa took one look at the happy group and decided to put an end to the discussion right away. With Stevie and Carole's boyfriends involved, there was no telling how much time this group would spend kidding around. "It's a long story," she said, trying to sound both pleasant and authoritative, "and unfortunately we don't have time to tell it."

"Let me guess, you're the stable manager, right?" Cam said.

"You got it," Lisa said. "And I've got a brown gelding with four white socks first up for inspection. With all this mud he'll have four black socks!"

"Hey! Don't forget A.J.'s horse is gray—all over," Phil pointed out, referring to their team member's Connemara mare. "We practically had to throw her in the washing machine and bleach out the grass stains—and all for nothing! If there was any justice in this world, they'd call this place *Rainy and Muddy* Valley Pony Club!"

Everyone laughed. Then Horse Wise and Cross County teams introduced their team members who didn't know each other and agreed to meet after the closing ceremony, which would take place late that afternoon.

"All right, until then—and may the best club win,"

Phil pronounced. He and Stevie exchanged looks. The two were known for their competitive spirits.

"Humph, we all know who that is," she said, sticking her nose in the air.

As SOON AS the girls got back to the stable area, Lisa posted the day's schedule, with the Horse Wise inspection and riding times highlighted. All of the inspections were about twenty minutes apart, and the dressage tests started right afterward. It was time to pick up the pace.

Lisa began delegating tasks right and left. If she didn't get everyone going, they would stay where they were—sitting on hay bales and complaining about the rain. "All right, Polly, you're first. Go and get dressed. Stevie and I will get Romeo out and go to work. Carole, you and Betsy start grooming Barq. Then, when Polly's gone, Stevie will start on Starlight. I'll final-check everyone before you go, so don't leave before I see you."

As Lisa spoke, two women in tweeds and mackintosh rain jackets stood by, listening intently. They made a couple of marks on their clipboards, nodded to the team, and went away. Lisa gulped. *Judges*, she thought, and she knew they'd be back when she least expected it.

The inspections flew by in a haze of activity. Betsy forgot her Pony Club pin, and Lisa had to chase her down. Then Carole couldn't find her stock tie. It had somehow gotten lost between Pine Hollow and Sunny

Valley. Lisa ran and caught Polly just finishing her inspection, practically ripped her tie off her neck, and charged back to tie it onto Carole's. Meanwhile she kept a running total of the Horse Wise deductions. At the end of tack and turnout, they'd been deducted for Polly and Betsy's dry stirrup leathers—all the cleaning in the world didn't take the place of regular oiling and care; Prancer's knobby chestnuts—Stevie was squeamish about picking them off; a stone in Starlight's hoof—unknown to Carole, he must have picked it up on the way over; and the boot polish on the inside of Carole's boots—it could rub off on her saddle and make black marks.

Carole felt a little bad that she and Starlight had messed up two things until she found out that she, Lisa (without any last-minute quizzing in the car), and Cam had received the only three perfect written test scores. It also cheered her up to see Veronica's name on the "50% or More Wrong" list. She passed Cam on the way back from the scoreboards and gave him the thumbs-up sign.

When it was time for the first set of dressage tests, it had started to rain so hard that keeping neat was practically impossible. Lisa shined everyone's boots, nevertheless, and sent them off as spotless as she could manage. She stayed behind to make sure the stable area ran smoothly. One by one they came back, soaked, bedraggled, and totally unsure of how they had done.

"I'm not even sure the judge could *see* my test, let alone be able to grade it," Stevie said. "Poor Prancer slid right both halts. I guess she held up pretty well, though, considering that we've never been out in a tidal wave before. I think in her past life she must have been a 'mudder'—you know, those racehorses who like a wet, slippery track."

"I can't say the same for Starlight," Carole said. They had all stripped off their wet clothes, hayed the horses, and sat down underneath the gray-and-green Horse Wise banner to wolf down Mrs. Reg's ham-and-cheese sandwiches. "He kept his ears pinned back the entire time. Actually, he looked so mad to be out in this weather that it made me crack up, and then I was totally relaxed."

"Barq couldn't believe we were out there, either," Betsy said. "The poor guy wishes he were back on the desert sands with his Arabian ancestors."

Polly was the only one who actually felt good about her ride. Perky, steady Romeo had proved himself a real trouper and hadn't seemed to mind the rain at all. "You're the best, aren't you?" Polly said, getting up to give him a hug.

Lisa refused to let the others check the scores after lunch. Instead, she told them to talk each other through their second dressage tests, which, judging from the clearing skies, would matter a whole lot more. By herself

127

she darted up to the fence where they were posted. She could barely read the numbers through the rain-coated plastic covering, but one thing was clear: The bad weather had kept everyone very close. Sunny Valley was in the lead, as Mrs. Reg had predicted, but a group of four teams, including Horse Wise and Cross County, were hot on the trail and well within striking distance. None of the stable-management scores had been added up yet. Individually, Polly and Romeo were in the top ten, as were Cam on Duffy, and Phil on Teddy. Stevie, Betsy, and Carole had all scored in the top half. Lisa took a few quick notes in case it came down to the wire. Then she went to get the crew ready. Running back through the drizzle, she saw Mrs. Reg, Max, and Colonel Hanson going up to check the scores themselves.

"Keep up the good work, Lisa!" Max yelled. Lisa vowed silently that she would.

In the afternoon there was a little bit more time between Horse Wise rides, so the stable managers could sneak out and watch after getting their next riders ready. Polly and Romeo put in another good, solid ride. They weren't spectacular, but they got the job done. Betsy had more trouble on Barq. The Arabian still seemed annoyed about the footing, and he went around looking stiff and unbalanced. One of the nicest tests Lisa saw was Cam's. He sat quietly and let Duffy strut his stuff. They had obviously been working hard. As Lisa gave Carole's stirrup irons a final swipe, she crossed her fingers that Starlight would look equally polished.

"ONE-TWO, ONE-TWO, LIKE a metronome. One-two," Carole repeated to herself as she circled the ring. The rain had finally stopped entirely, and she could feel her hands sweating. Swallowing hard, she made herself sit up straighter and think about everything Max and Stevie and Starlight had been telling her—not only for the past two weeks but for the past year. She took a deep breath. She patted Starlight's neck, entered at a working trot, and saluted.

From her vantage point on the slope beside the ring, Lisa watched as the two put in their best test ever. Starlight wasn't transformed into a perfect dressage horse— he still didn't bend around the corners—but he paid attention to Carole.

"Accurate, steady, rhythmical—all the fundamentals are there," Lisa said to herself happily. Out of the corner of her eye, she glimpsed Cam holding Duffy. He gave Lisa a grin that told her he was thinking the same thing.

Stevie was the last Horse Wise rider to go and one of the last riders of the day. The whole team came out to watch. A few minutes before she started, Phil and Cam appeared, along with their friend A.J. If Stevie noticed her fan club, she didn't show it. She rode her test calmly and methodically. When Prancer got silly, Stevie corrected her right away. When she wanted to go too fast, Stevie steadied her with her hands and seat. As they came down the center line for the second time, Horse Wise let out a collective sigh of relief. They had done it: The Thoroughbred mare off the track and the determined junior rider had competed successfully at a Pony Club event. Before she could dismount, Horse Wise, Cross County, and both teams' parents and coaches had surrounded Stevie in a cheering crowd.

IN THE STATION wagon on the way home, the girls ate two boxes of leftover cookies and rehashed the entire day, from waking up and seeing black skies to riding en masse to collect their third-place-team ribbons.

"I think the best part for me was watching Cam get second overall," Carole said dreamily.

"That's the difference between you two and us two," Stevie said. "For me it was bad enough seeing Cross County win the whole darn thing, but if Phil had gotten an individual ribbon today, I probably would have had to go on a hunger strike."

"Better Cross County than Sunny Valley," Polly pointed out. She was stretched out way in the back of the wagon, gazing at her fifth-place-overall ribbon.

"Amen to that!" Stevie agreed. "Too bad Veronica's written test and messy stall dropped them down to second place."

"I can't wait to tell Lisa that they lost on stable management," Carole said. As soon as Stevie had finished her test, Lisa had run off to meet her mother's waiting car. Dress rehearsal began at seven, and she had to be completely costumed and made up by six-fifteen.

"And I can't wait even more to tell her about the special stable-management award we got," Stevie added.

Carole thought for a minute. "You know what I can't wait for the most? To see Lisa onstage."

"Me, too," Stevie agreed. "And we only have two hours to go."

LATER THAT EVENING Stevie and Carole took their seats in the small family-and-friends-only WCCT dress-rehearsal audience. They didn't quite know what to expect, but they hoped Lisa would do well. Far from being disappointed, they were quite blown away by the whole play, and most especially by Lisa's performance. She acted, sang, and danced her way through the musical as if she'd played Annie a hundred times. Stevie and Carole literally sat on the edges of their seats, trying to catch every word and clapping like crazy after every one of Lisa's solos.

After the rehearsal they went backstage to congratulate her. Lisa was surrounded by the rest of the cast. Stevie and Carole had never felt as proud as they did right then to be Lisa's best friends. Lisa looked up from the theater group and saw them standing there.

"You were an incredible Annie, and we got a special stable-management award, and Sunny Valley PC lost because of Veronica!" Stevie cried, unable to contain herself any longer.

All of a sudden it got quiet. The cast stared at Stevie's strange announcement. Then Lisa's joyful shout broke the silence. "Yippee!" she yelled. "We did it!" She broke through the crowd to embrace her two friends.

"You must be Stevie and Carole," Hollie said, coming up to introduce herself.

Carole smiled at the warm face and pretty brown curls. "And you must be Hollie—it's great to meet you."

"Want to go to TD's, Little Orphan Annie?" Stevie asked.

Lisa nodded happily. She was exhausted, but she wouldn't miss going for anything.

"Hollie, will you come, too?" Stevie asked.

Hollie declined politely. "Actually, I do have to get home tonight," she said. "I'd love to come another time, but I have to say I'm a little nervous about watching you eat your famous sundae concoctions."

"You should be," Carole told her. "Going up onstage in front of hundreds of strangers can't be half as terrifying as watching what goes down her throat."

* * *

IT DIDN'T TAKE long for The Saddle Club to get from the high school to TD's, and it took even less time for them to slide into their favorite booth.

"Well, I'll be darned. She *looks* like your old friend—sort of," the waitress said, looking Lisa up and down.

In their hurry to have a true Saddle Club reunion, Carole and Stevie had talked Lisa into leaving on all of her makeup and most of her costume. In the dimmer lighting she looked like a painted doll. Comments from the waitress weren't going to get to them tonight, though.

"This is her evil twin," Stevie shot back. "By the way, would you mind getting out a pencil to take my order? It's going to be extremely complex, as I finally have my appetite back."

The waitress smiled and grabbed the pencil from behind her ear. "Okay, shoot," she said. "I'm actually kind of looking forward to this."

Stevie grinned wickedly. "All right. Make mine one scoop each of peaches 'n' cream, peppermint bonbon, and orange sherbet, drenched in chocolate, butterscotch, blueberry, and cherry syrups, topped with whipped cream, Butterfinger crunch, Oreo cookie sprinkles, chocolate sprinkles, shredded coconut, a sliced banana, six sliced strawberries, and, of course, a maraschino cherry."

The waitress looked up from her pad. She rolled her

eyes. She shook her head. Then she took Carole and Lisa's orders: a vanilla-and-chocolate swirl and a mint chip with hot fudge. "That's more like it," she muttered, going to fix the grossest Stevie Lake concoction yet.

The girls could hardly start gabbing fast enough. Maybe because they hadn't had a real Saddle Club discussion for so long, the conversation took on a serious tone. They talked about being good at a lot of things versus being interested in only one, about making choices and balancing commitments. Lisa told Stevie that she thought the most generous thing she did was to give Prancer the experience of riding in the rally.

"I didn't do it for Prancer, though," Stevie said. "I did it for myself. I was getting a real swelled head about being so good on Topside. And we all know humility isn't my strong suit."

Lisa looked at her skeptically. "You really want me to believe you rode her to teach *yourself* a lesson?" she asked.

Stevie had plenty of time to think about her answer. The waitress arrived with their ice creams and gave Carole and Lisa their dishes. Stevie's had too much stuff in it to fit in a regular bowl. The waitress hadn't let that bother her, though. She had dumped everything into a metal dishwashing tub. She set the tub down in front of Stevie.

"Just do me a favor, okay?"

"Anything," Stevie promised.

"Don't let me see the look on your face when you finish eating that thing."

Digging in happily, Stevie gave her word between mouthfuls. Finally she paused to respond to Lisa's question. "I admit—disciplining myself wasn't my real motive for riding Prancer," she conceded.

"What, then?" Lisa asked.

"It was to do something for you—because you needed a friend," Stevie said simply.

Lisa put her spoon down with a clink. "I've got the two best friends in the world, and you don't have to lift a finger to prove it ever again. Just do *me* one favor, okay? Remind me occasionally that even though I like doing a lot of things, I can't do them all at once or I'll mess one of them up for sure."

"Sure, Lisa. I'll remind you when I call to recongratulate you on the stable-management award, that is," Carole said. She pretended to be lost in thought for a minute. Then she said pensively, "The call will come at, let's say, nine forty-four."

"But—" Lisa objected.

"Nine forty-four," Carole repeated. "Exactly."

ABOUT THE AUTHOR

BONNIE BRYANT is the author of more than sixty books for young readers, including novelizations of movie hits such as *Teenage Mutant Ninja Turtles®* and *Honey, I Blew Up the Kid*, written under her married name, B. B. Hiller.

Ms. Bryant began writing The Saddle Club in 1986. Although she had done some riding before that, she intensified her studies then and found herself learning right along with her characters Stevie, Carole, and Lisa. She claims that they are all much better riders than she is.

Ms. Bryant was born and raised in New York City. She lives in Greenwich Village with her two sons.

Saddle Up For Fun!
Join The Saddle Club

As an official Saddle Club member you'll get:

- *Saddle Club newsletter*
- *Saddle Club membership card*
- *Saddle Club bookmark*
- *and exciting updates on everything that's happening with your favorite series.*

Bantam Doubleday Dell Books for Young Readers
Saddle Club Membership Box BK
1540 Broadway
New York, NY 10036

SKYLARK

Bantam Doubleday Dell
Books for Young Readers

Name _____

Address _____

City _____ State _____ Zip _____

Age _____

Offer good while supplies last.   BFYR - 8/93